picture perfect

picture perfect

elaine marie alphin

Carolrhoda Books, Inc. • Minneapolis

Carolrhoda Books, Inc.
A division of Lerner Publishing Group
241 First Avenue North
Minneapolis, MN 55401 U.S.A.

Website address: www.lernerbooks.com

Library of Congress Cataloging-in-Publication Data

Alphin, Elaine Marie.
    Picture perfect / by Elaine Marie Alphin.
        p.   cm.
    Summary: A gap in his memory the afternoon that his best friend
disappears in a redwood forest has a fifteen-year-old photographer wondering
about his own role in the mystery, and who he can turn to for help.
    ISBN-13: 978–0–8225–0535–8 (lib. bdg. : alk. paper)
    ISBN-10: 0–8225–0535–5 (lib. bdg. : alk. paper)
    [1. Missing persons—Fiction. 2. Fathers and sons—Fiction.
3. Photography—Fiction. 4. Schools—Fiction. 5. Psychological abuse—
Fiction. 6. California—Fiction.] I. Title.
PZ7.A4625Pi 2003
[Fic]—dc21   2002154241

Manufactured in the United States of America
4 5 6 7 8 9 – BP – 11 10 09 08 07 06

For Pam,
who shares my love of the redwoods

for Art,
who sees the truth behind the image

and for Shannon,
without whom Ian's story
might never have come into focus

in the dream forest

I see him falling away from me, into the fog. Towering redwood trunks surround me like majestic pillars in some otherworldly cathedral, pushing me back, keeping me from him. I hear the dull thumps his body makes hitting the duff-covered slope, and rushing water beyond the trees. I open my mouth, but the forest presses in on me, deadening my shouts as it has deadened his.

I strain to push past the largest redwood separating me from him. It holds me back, the rough, shaggy bark scraping my cheek. I wrap my arms as far around the tree as they will go, but they barely reach halfway. The streaked bark is damp as I scrub my face against it, trying to dry the tears, not knowing whether it's the tree crying or me. Overhead, a spotted owl hoots once in outrage, and I wake up.

I reach automatically for the alarm clock, still sleep-dazed by dream images unfolding like a series of photos—except for the sounds and feelings, of course. You can show a lot in a photograph, but you can't recreate the sound of an owl or water (or his body), or the feel of tree bark against your cheek or soft, woody duff underfoot. But those were just sensations between dreaming and waking—the owl's hoot was only the alarm. I fumble to push the switch and re-alize I'm not in bed, with the clock on the table beside me. I'm in the closet under the stairs.

It's just a storage closet—unpainted planks, uncarpeted floor, with a strangely shaped door that fits the slope of the stairs above. Some people might use it to store a vacuum cleaner, but it has another purpose in Dad's house. I don't remember coming down here. Was I sleepwalking again last night? Sometimes I get all the way outdoors, but usu-ally I only make it as far as the closet. I shut myself inside, curl up, and slide back into deep sleep again. I must have done that, maybe while I was dreaming. I can't be sure.

Sometimes I think I remember how things happened, but then Dad says that's not the way it was. Or he gives me a strange, sidelong look, and says it never happened at all and asks if I dreamed it. I feel off-kilter when he does that, like I'm walking in the forest and the duff slides down the slope underfoot without warning, and I'm falling into an eroded crevice or a hidden streambed, helpless to catch myself. I want to remember things the way Dad says they were, so the world won't tilt and dump me.

Maybe it isn't important why I slept in the closet. I just hurry upstairs and get ready for school. It bothers me a lit-tle that my cheek looks red and creased in the mirror as I brush my teeth, but I must have been leaning the left side of my face against the closet wall—that's all. When I go downstairs as quietly as possible, I'm relieved to see Dad has already gone and Mom's back in bed.

I take the time to toast a bagel and eat it with cream cheese and some juice while I read the comics and flip through the rest of the paper. I only glance at the sports section—the school jocks haven't made news lately, so I don't have any photos there. Dad's already seen the paper and it's okay for me to read it, but just in case he looks again when he gets home I'm careful not to crease the pages.

After carefully washing the plate and knife and glass I used, and putting them away, I heft my backpack and head for the side door to put on shoes. On the scrubbed outdoor carpet lining the little room where we leave jackets and shoes, I see the hiking boots I usually wear, half kicked under the row of coats and jackets—their soles caked with dried woody duff from the forest floor.

I stare at the boots, rubbing my sore cheek. *Please, no.*

tuesday: missing

The moment Mrs. Camden opens her front door, I know Teddy's not there.

But I push the thought away before it can take root. He's just running late. That's all. It's my fault—I biked too fast to his house and didn't give him enough time. I'll hear him clattering down the stairs any minute.

"Is Teddy ready for school yet?" I ask, as if nothing is wrong, as if Mrs. Camden isn't standing there in rumpled sweats, her blonde hair tangled, already drunk at 7:45 in the morning. "We're going to be late," I add.

She stands there, staring blearily at me from her cluttered hallway. "Ian?" she croaks. "I called you last night— when Teddy didn't come home for supper. I called to ask if he was at your place."

I swallow, the memory of the call flooding back into me—Dad's anger at his phone ringing for me—him standing over me, glaring at me to get off the line fast. I say, uncertainly, "You mean, he didn't get back until later."

She shakes her head impatiently, loose strands of hair falling into her eyes. "Never got back at all! My Teddy's gone." She drags the last word out until it dissolves into tears, and I want to hug her and promise everything's going to be okay, Teddy's okay, but I'm no good at hugging, so I just stand there.

You hear about kids going missing on the evening news, in places like San Francisco, but not in a little town like Sawville. Nothing happens here. There's barely enough news to fill the daily paper. I think they only publish it every day because they used to when the lumber business was booming, before this land all got named a state park. Teddy couldn't have gone missing in Sawville.

Maybe he just stayed at our hideout overnight for some reason. Or maybe he couldn't take his mom yelling at him like she does sometimes when she drinks, and decided to camp out. It's just that he's never done that before. The dream memory of a body's muffled thumps as it falls toward rushing water hits me, and I feel dizzy. *Please, Teddy— you've got to be all right.*

"You were with him," Mrs. Camden says suddenly. She's stopped crying, and her voice sounds accusing. "What did you two do after school? Where did you go?"

My stomach cramps, and I wish I hadn't eaten that bagel. "I didn't do anything with him," I tell her. "He took off after school on his bike."

"You went with him," she insisted. "You must have— you two are always together!"

"We were supposed to hang out in the forest," I admit, unsure what to tell her. Teddy's the only one I can talk to easily. I flounder on, "We were going to take some pictures—"

She snorts. "More tree pictures! Waste of time . . . "

The criticism sears me for a second, but I tell myself she

doesn't mean it. No matter what she says when she's drunk about our wasting time and money on redwood photos, I know she's got a bunch of Teddy's pictures hanging on the living room wall in cheap plastic frames.

"He went off on his own," I tell her. "I waited for him, but he never showed up. I didn't even take any pictures." For once it doesn't matter that I can't find the right words—she doesn't hear me. Tears are running down her cheeks from unfocused eyes.

I look past the entrance hallway, packed with rickety furniture and boxes of stuff she hasn't decided what to do with, at the wall behind her. There's the photo I took of Teddy and his mother at the beach last summer, both of them grinning. She'd been sober the day I took the picture, and she'd acted younger, more like a big sister than a mother, her round face pink and laughing under her bleached blonde hair as she hugged him from behind. And Teddy hadn't been worried about anything—you could see that in the way his grin stretched all the way up into his clear gray eyes. Photos don't lie, and this one shimmers with happiness the way the ocean behind them shimmers in the sun.

"What are you looking at?" she demands, her voice hoarse.

"The picture of you two," I say. My voice is only a little shaky. "You both look so happy." I'd felt like an outsider watching the two of them—glad to see their joy, but wishing Mom had come to the beach with me that day, so I'd feel like part of a family, too. "Teddy's going to turn up," I tell her helplessly. "He's got to."

She turns and squints at the picture, and starts to cry

again. "I called the sheriff's office. They said he's run off. My Teddy wouldn't run off."

I know he wouldn't. At least, not without telling me. And taking me with him.

"They said they can't do anything until he's gone for twenty-four hours, because he's over ten. What's that got to do with it?"

It's getting close to eight. I'm going to be late for school if I don't hurry. It's out of my way to pick up Teddy, but I bike the extra three-quarters of a mile to his house every morning because I don't want him to come get me. Dad always says he sees enough kids at school all day—he doesn't want extra kids running around his house.

"I've got to go, Mrs. Camden," I mumble, heading for the bike I'd dropped on her front lawn. I lift it, but it slips through unsteady fingers and thuds down on the grass. I pick it up again and look back at her. "Maybe he'll be at school, and come home this afternoon to tell you all about some big adventure."

"If he does, so help me—" she begins, her fists clenched. Then she bites back the rest of what she wanted to say and shakes her head. "I'm calling the sheriff again. And your father. He's the principal—if Teddy's not in school, I'll make him call the truant officer if the sheriff won't do anything."

The door bangs shut behind her, and I bike to school, pumping leaden pedals, no breath in my chest. I focus on the effort of biking, trying hard not to think about her calling Dad (how could she *make* him do anything?), trying hard not to miss Teddy's presence beside me, trying to be the person I am when I'm with Teddy—more confident, more hopeful, even happy sometimes.

For almost three years he's been there. Teddy lives on the south side of Sawville, far enough away that he was in a different elementary school. But since we started middle school he's pedaled beside me to classes, then off to our hideout, or to the library or a movie, and back home again, every day except when he got the measles and stayed home for a week. We're like brothers—I'd know if Teddy had been planning something. Wouldn't I?

I can't remember Teddy saying anything about what he'd had in mind, but now I recall Mrs. Camden's call more clearly. She'd sounded sharp rather than drunk. Teddy hates it when she drinks. He says she drinks to forget his dad leaving, only it makes her remember more, not less. When she gets drunk, she tells him he's just like his dad. Sometimes she tells him she wishes he were dead. Then she'll start crying, and say that isn't true—she's sorry—she loves him—she'd even loved his dad.

"I know she means it," Teddy would say. In my mind's snapshot I can see him running one hand through his frizzy dark red hair and looking weighed down with more worries than a fourteen-year-old should have to handle—like he got stuck playing the role of the parent instead of just being a kid. "She goes on about how she's so glad she has me and I'm worth ten of my dad. But then she says it's just the booze talking when she says I'm like my dad, and I'm not so sure—I think, maybe, she means that too. I think, maybe, she's mad at him and me both."

He'd pause and look off into space. "And sometimes I think—if only my dad were here, maybe he'd know what to do with her." But Teddy didn't know who his dad was. His

mom would never tell him, and after a while he quit asking. I know he still thought about it.

Then, just as I'd be about to tell him exactly how well
I understood the way he felt so helpless, Teddy would shrug
and grin. "Hey—everybody can't have a happy family with
two parents like you do, can they? Come on, Ian—we're
losing light. Let's snap some shots!"

And I'd bike off after him into the forest, my backpack
thudding heavily with each jolt of the wheels over the uneven duff, glad I'd kept quiet. Teddy never stays down for
long, no matter what. He has to be okay now, like he's always been. I'll turn around any minute, and there he'll be,
and everything will be fine, like yesterday.

But when I get to the school bike rack, there's no sign
of his scuffed-up bike. I take a deep breath before plunging
into the crowded hallways, trying to become the "at-school
Ian," the smart, confident kid the teachers expect me to be,
even if the students don't buy it.

When you're the principal's son other kids figure you're
a brain—or so dumb you'll flunk out unless Dad makes the
teachers fork over passes. Either way, they expect you to be
too stuck up to make friends, except with brownnosers who
want to suck up to the principal. No one was surprised I
won that essay contest last year, not even Teddy—and especially not Dad, since it was the chance he'd been waiting
for to have me do something really great so he could brag
about his successful son.

When I'm with Teddy, it's easier to be the school Ian
I'm supposed to be. He's confident enough for both of us.
Kids see him and yell "Hi!" and he high-fives guys I barely
recognize. Some of them shoot me grins as if they know me

or even like me. I grin back, but I'm not fooled into thinking they could be friends.

Today a couple of kids call, "Hey, Ian! Where's Teddy?" but I don't know what to say so I just shrug. The rest ignore me. I do hear a few spurts of laughter, and flush, sure they're laughing at me. I try to walk like I belong, the way I stride along beside Teddy, and after awhile I'm doing it. I've turned into the school Ian that other people recognize, even if they don't like him much.

I don't care what any of them think, anyway, only Teddy. And, I guess, maybe Sara Wyatt and Mr. Mitchell. But they don't really know me—not the way Teddy does. I try not to think about all the things Teddy doesn't know about me as I turn down another corridor. For a second I look up, hoping to see him leaning against his locker, talking to Sara about the yearbook, but no one's there. Just a crowd of strangers, slamming lockers and pushing their way through the halls.

Then I open the locker I use, right beside his, and reach into my backpack to switch books for the morning's class— and my hand comes out of my pack with Teddy's digital camera, its red light blinking plaintively to announce the battery is dead.

special assembly

I shove the camera into the locker, grab a notebook and the book I'll need for core English and history, and slam the metal door shut, hoping nobody saw. How did Teddy's camera get in my backpack? I don't think he left the camera with me yesterday afternoon, before he took off. Did he come back to the hideout without my seeing him somehow, and put it in my backpack? But why?

I head blindly for homeroom and sit numbly while Ms. Francis takes attendance and the intercom blares static-choked announcements I can't decipher. When the bell rings, I start to head for Mr. Mitchell's class, then realize the other kids are getting in line to go somewhere as a group. I fall in at the back, wondering what I missed. Was something special scheduled for today?

"Ian!" Sara whispers impatiently. She's the editor of the school newspaper and the yearbook, both. I met her the first day of seventh grade, when I went to ask the publications adviser if I could maybe be the newspaper's photographer.

The adviser turned out to be Mr. Mitchell, and he'd already made Sara editor. Teddy was there first, asking if he could do the photographs. I would have expected most kids to just tell me to get lost so they could have the job. If he'd done that, I'd have gone away. But Teddy didn't even say, "You be the newspaper photographer and I'll be the year-book photographer." He just lit up and said, "Cool! Let's work together!" Mr. Mitchell said that would be fine, and Sara beamed at both of us and wrote down our names.

Now she joins the line beside me and asks softly, "Where's Teddy?"

Her voice sounds stuffy and nasal, and the name comes out more like "Deddy." She sighs. "Spring cold. I always get them this time of year."

I nod automatically, wondering what it would be like to get sick and miss the forest coming alive. "Where are we going?" I ask stupidly, noticing the other classes filing into the hallway along with ours.

"There's a special assembly," Sara says, "about Teddy. Didn't you hear the intercom?" So that's what the static had said. She pauses, her plump face worried behind her tinted glasses, a soft purple that screens out sunlight and probably most of the school fluorescent lights as well. The lenses make her eyes look wider, and faintly purple and mysterious as well. "Ian, do you know what happened to him?"

I shake my head, following her to the auditorium, wondering what Dad plans to do at this assembly. "Teddy went off on his own after school yesterday," I tell her. "Then his mom called me last night to ask if he was with me. When I went by to get him this morning, she said he still hadn't come home."

Sara frowns, hugging her backpack to her chest instead of slinging it over her shoulders. "I wonder what he was up to." She sneezes and fumbles in her pack for a tissue. "Sorry. Didn't he say anything to you?"

"We just planned to shoot some redwood pictures," I tell her, the way I told Teddy's mother. "But he never showed up."

Sara eyes my bulky backpack, not needing laser vision by now to know I've got my own camera inside it along with my laptop for downloading pictures. "How come you guys are always out in the forest taking pictures of trees and ferns and stuff? What about the yearbook and the newspaper?"

I look at her, suddenly worried that I've missed a deadline. Sara's the one person other than Teddy who actually treats me like a friend, and I don't want to disappoint her. "There's nothing for the newspaper right now, is there? And I thought I was on schedule with yearbook pictures— did I mess up?"

"No, you're not behind—and your stuff is great," Sara says, surprising me. Even though I try hard, my pictures don't usually come out the way I see them in my mind. Teddy's are much better. "It's just—I don't understand why you two take so many pictures of trees instead of people."

I shrug, not trying to explain. To me the redwoods are solid—more trustworthy than people. It's peaceful in the forest. You sort of feel you've stepped out of time, into a magic world where you're safe, where nothing can hurt you. The redwoods are terrible, and wonderful—God's trees, not like the little trees people plant in their yards, or even the tan oaks that grow in the redwoods' shade. I feel protected in the forest, surrounded by trees that have survived for a thousand years—some longer. It's safer photographing trees than people, too. Trees don't have anything to hide, secret layers that only emerge in photos.

And Teddy always says he loves the challenge of photographing the trees because of the shade and the forest fog. "If I can get the settings just right," he says, "I can get the shafts of sunlight slanting between the trees." He's written a bunch of different macro scripts—camera shortcuts to change the settings based on lighting conditions, as well as computer program macros to run photography applications. He offered to set my camera up the same way, but I'm just not clever enough to understand the scripting like he does. I guess I do the settings by feel, or instinct, or something. But I let Teddy load his macros onto my iBook, since he uses it all the time. And I got him to show me how to run some of the simpler shortcuts, ones I could remember, even if I don't understand how they work, for faster application set-ups. Those help me a lot.

Sara brushes her curling bangs off her forehead with the hand clutching the tissue. I've always wanted to tell her how pretty her hair is, but I've never quite dared. She treats me like a friend, but she's probably never even considered me as boyfriend material—Teddy's the one she likes that way, I'm sure. It's safer just to take a picture of her hair curling in the damp spring air. If she doesn't like it, she can blame the picture instead of the photographer. Seeing me studying her, she says, "Hey—what's that bruise on your cheek?"

I rub the sore spot, dismayed. If she can see it, is everyone else wondering about it too? I make myself shrug casually and come up with a plausible excuse. "Don't know. Maybe I bumped into a branch or something yesterday afternoon when I was thinking about framing a photograph."

I didn't take any pictures yesterday, but Sara doesn't know that.

"You sure can lose yourself in your pictures," she says. "Well, I wish you'd been with Teddy instead of shooting photos on your own."

"Me too," I say, and mean it.

In the auditorium I slide into the second row beside Sara. I slump down on the scuffed and creaking wooden seat, wishing I were shorter so I could hide behind the student sitting in front of me. There's no point in continuing the conversation here. The other kids are making so much noise we'd have to shout to hear each other, and I'd just get in trouble for being loud. If you're the principal's son, you have to be twice as good as any other kid, even if you're lucky enough to have an understanding dad. Besides, Sara's rummaging in her pack for paper to take notes. She never stops being a journalist. I guess she can't help but know there's a big article in this for the school paper. I'd be interested in reading it myself, if it were about someone other than Teddy.

My father strides down the wide auditorium steps, a tall, stocky man with muscles from working out and a broad grin that wins over even kids who don't like school. I find myself smiling in admiration—and wishing I could pull it off as well as he does. Dad really comes across like the perfect principal he wants to be. I worked so hard to find the school Ian this morning that I see Dad's public image clearly today, too. He's one person here and one person at home. I guess everyone is one person in private and somebody else when they're with other people. But not everybody's as good at it as Dad.

He towers above the students, all dressed in variations of the school dress code—dark blue slacks or skirts, some sort of white shirt, blue sweaters or sweatshirts. Dad wears a dark blue suit with a starched white shirt, acting like he's one of the gang. He speaks to a couple of kids along the way, and they laugh with him and quit talking to each other, obeying him willingly. Then he climbs the steps to the auditorium stage, flicks the switch on the mike, and raps it. I jump, along with the handful of kids who hadn't seen him yet.

"Settle down, now," Dad says. He's got a warm, carrying voice with a hint of humor that echoes through the hallways. The auditorium sound system's deep reverberations make it sound like the mesmerizing voice of a preacher. The kids quiet fairly quickly.

"I'm sure you know why I've called this assembly," Dad goes on, exchanging the warm humor for regretful concern. "Teddy Camden didn't come home after school yesterday." There's a brief flurry of whispers. Beside me, Sara scowls under her brown bangs and scrubs at her nose with the tissue.

"This is a very serious situation," he goes on, "and I've asked someone to come in this morning who can explain it to you best." He pauses, looking toward the back of the auditorium while most of the kids crane their necks around to see what's going on. When the volume of whispering shoots up, I turn and see Mrs. Camden wobbling down the aisle, hanging onto Mrs. Feeney, the school secretary, to hold herself upright.

"You know Teddy's mother, Mrs. Camden." There's more whispering, and Dad smiles faintly as she walks unsteadily up to the microphone. She's changed into a skirt and sweater, and tried to fix her hair. She looks a lot better than she did in her sweats a little while ago, but her skirt hangs crooked and I wince when I see the edge of her slip drooping down on one side.

I remember her saying she'd call Dad. What pressure did she put on him to make him call this assembly? I can tell he doesn't really want to be up there, even if the other kids don't realize it.

"Please," Dad tells her, stepping back and gesturing to the mike stand.

She blinks at the crowded auditorium for a minute, then bends too close to the mike. "My Teddy—" she begins, and the microphone lets out a high-pitched shriek.

The kids laugh, and Dad steps forward. "Okay people—it's just the sound system. Now listen to Mrs. Camden."

She glares at him through narrowed eyes, as if the electric scream was his fault, then looks back at the mike suspiciously. "My Teddy," she starts again, standing a little way back from it this time, "didn't come home last night. He was in school yesterday, so you all saw him then. But something must have happened to him."

She's speaking slowly and carefully so her words won't slur—she can't have sobered up completely since I saw her earlier. She swallows and goes on, "I'm hoping some of you know what he did yesterday, or what he was planning to do, maybe. Or maybe you saw him meet someone." She looks down, and I'm close enough to see her eyes fill with tears. Beside me, Sara frowns, sniffles, then goes back to scribbling notes.

Mrs. Camden says, her voice so low the microphone

barely picks it up, "My Teddy was—was—" She takes a deep breath, and her voice booms out of the mike, "—looking for his father."

Her face flushes in dark red blotches, and a couple of kids giggle nervously.

She frowns at them, and reaches out and grabs the microphone stand with one hand, ignoring the deep, hollow bang the sound system makes. "Okay—you—I know what your parents think of me, but if one of you was missing, they'd sure want my Teddy to tell them anything he knew! So if you heard him talking about going away somewhere with somebody, or saw him talking to any man, or getting in a car with anybody, you got to tell me." Now the tears spill down her face. "Please."

There's an explosion of whispers, and she turns around and looks at Dad, her face angry again through the tears. Dad studies us for a minute, letting everyone quiet down, then steps up to the microphone. "Thank you, Mrs. Camden. Now—I know you kids feel that what you tell each other is a sacred trust, never to be divulged to an adult." Dad smiles. "I've got a son of my own here, and I know that's the way he feels."

Actually, between being embarrassed for Mrs. Camden and mortified for myself, what I really feel like is slipping down between the seats and dissolving into the floor. But I just sit there, listening as the kids release the pent-up laughter they held back for Mrs. Camden. They don't mind dumping it on me. Sara's not laughing, however. She leans over and whispers, "I don't think your father should have let Teddy's mom get up there like that."

I glance at Sara, but she's busy scribbling again. It's not

Dad's fault Mrs. Camden's drunk. He was only trying to help her—I'm surprised Sara doesn't see that. I feel Mrs. Camden looking at me, and I think hard about yesterday afternoon, but all I see is Teddy's smiling face as he set off after school, leaving me alone.

I've got to find some way to clear my mind and remember—if only I could be sure I wasn't missing anything, I'd feel better. I remember sitting in our hideout a little after 4:00, reading a photography magazine. And I remember writing in my journal around 5:30. But I can't see myself doing anything between 4:30 and 5:30.

Sometimes I sort of zone out—kind of like those Indian fakirs who go into a trance so they can walk on hot coals. I lose time in a fog when that happens, and I don't even remember if I've done things. Sometimes I've woken up somewhere without knowing how I got there, like the sleepwalking, but it's never a big deal. I mean, I've missed a class assignment now and then, and once I never realized Sara expected me to photograph a play rehearsal for the newspaper. She was kind of steamed, but I made it up in the next issue and she forgave me. This time, though, I really did miss something important—if I hadn't zoned out, maybe I'd have been there for Teddy.

"But there are times when a friend's safety outweighs that trust, and I'm afraid this is one of them," Dad goes on. His expression turns serious, his eyebrows drawing down in the middle of his forehead. Now that the kids have let off some steam, they're listening to him, believing him. "If any student knows anything about what Teddy Camden did yesterday after school, or if any student knows where Teddy Camden might be now, I would like that student to come talk to me after this assembly. This will be entirely confidential—no one will get into any trouble for helping us locate Teddy. Please remember that his mother is extremely distraught. It's important that she know the truth about her son." He's talking about her as if she's not standing there on the stage beside him.

Dad's eyes rove across the seated students—sincere, concerned. Then, without warning, I feel them boring into me. Behind the concern I see accusation, and I suddenly feel ice cold in the crowded, stuffy auditorium. Why is he staring at me like that?

Because you're Teddy's best friend, a soft, clear voice whispers, and I nearly jump out of the seat.

I shoot Sara a sideways glance to see if she heard the voice, but she's frowning up at the stage, chewing on the ragged thumbnail of her left hand. She didn't hear him, but she must feel my look because she turns.

"What?" Her whisper is completely different from the other one, a soft breath turned upward in a question, not a clear voice that echoes somewhere in the back of my head.

I want to ask, "Did you hear that?" But I can't seem to force the words out.

Yes, you can—ask her. The voice is no longer whispering. *Then tell her about me. Please.*

It's Luke.

I haven't heard him for so many years that I can scarcely believe it's him. And even though it seems impossible, his voice hasn't changed at all from the one I used to know so well.

Sara still doesn't react to him, only to me, her expression turning faintly puzzled. That's how it always was before. I was the only one who could hear him.

If you want to help Teddy, you can't do it alone, Luke insists, his voice more demanding. *Please, Ian—listen to me, or things are going to get worse.*

I wish Sara *could* hear him. Then I wouldn't have to decide what to do. Because I can't, not on my own. My chest feels tight and I can barely breathe. Sara's frown turns worried. "Are you okay?"

I manage to nod at her and force myself to inhale slowly, steadily, then exhale. Again. When I'm finally breathing almost like normal and she turns back to her notes, Luke whispers softly, *Please—you have to think about Teddy.*

I'm terrified for him!

No, you're not. Not yet, anyway. Luke sounds regretful, almost helpless. *When you're really more worried about Teddy than yourself, you'll listen to me. I know it's hard, Ian—but what happened to Teddy changes everything.*

I don't know what to think, and Luke falls silent.

Around me, in the assembly, the students are silent also. Finally, when none of them volunteer any information, Dad says, "You heard what Mrs. Camden is afraid of. I especially want to know if anyone saw a strange man hanging around school yesterday." He sighs. "I know you all think you're too old to worry about that 'stranger' stuff you're taught in elementary school, but the truth is that you're never too old to stop being careful around someone you don't know. If Teddy Camden trusted a stranger, thinking the man might be his father, and any of you saw anyone suspicious, I need to know as soon as possible so I can get the information to the sheriff."

Whispers erupt around the auditorium. Even the teachers are murmuring to each other in the back. Realization explodes inside me like a flash, but I don't let anyone see it, not even Sara.

Cal! The only strange man Teddy knew was Cal, and no one here will think of him because he wouldn't come anywhere near the school. But if Teddy needed help in the forest and couldn't reach me, he'd go to Cal. If I can find Cal after school, if he'll let me find him, if he'll talk to me—he might know something.

Dad raps the mike. "Okay, that's enough now. Look, people—I've been here at Sequoia Middle School for six years now, long enough that I know you all and I know your brothers and sisters who've gone on to high school, and I care about all of you."

The kids nod, smiling a little, distracted from worrying about Teddy. They like Dad being principal—the way he knows their names and jokes with them in the hallways. But I know he's not staying here, no matter how much he cares about his students. He's about to be promoted to the superintendent job he's wanted for as long as I can remember.

I was really looking forward to moving up to high school for tenth grade next year—riding the bus away from Sawville, going to a school where no one knows Dad, taking classes with Teddy and setting the school Ian free to explore who I really am, all day, the way I can behind a camera. But with Dad's promotion, I'll drive in with him. He'll be in and out of the high school all the time, always keeping his eye on me, watching out for me, and I'll go on being his less-than-perfect son—the superintendent's disappointing son instead of the principal's disappointing son, but that's no real difference. Nothing will change.

"That means I care about Teddy Camden," Dad continues, "and I intend to make sure we find him, safe and sound." He pauses a moment, then underscores his sincerity by adding, "A school is like a family—what happens to one member, student or faculty, affects everyone else, and I take the same personal interest in finding Teddy Camden as I would take in finding my own son."

A flash of alarm goes off inside me. Would the school board somehow blame Dad for not keeping track of his students, and pull the superintendent job? If they did—well, life at home wouldn't be worth living. I look up at Mrs. Camden standing forlornly on the stage, her slip hanging unevenly, her eyes bright with tears. It's bad enough worrying about Teddy and his mother—now I'm worrying about Dad and our family, too. Somehow I've got to find a way to remember what happened yesterday, and then do something about it—starting with Cal.

Dad scans the silent auditorium. "I'll be contacting the sheriff, and I'll be in my office all morning, waiting. I hope that any student who knows anything at all about Teddy Camden will come see me as soon as possible."

He lets the words hang there in the microphone's echo for a moment and looks straight at me. Then he finishes, "Let's all pull together on this one, people. Thank you."

He flicks the microphone off, turns, and motions Mrs. Camden down the steps ahead of him. She staggers slightly but pulls away when he offers her a hand, so he just follows her off the stage and up the aisle.

Sara turns to me, her plump face serious. "Can't you remember anything Teddy said or did yesterday? Even if you think it's not important, something you guys did might mean something to Mrs. Camden, or to the sheriff." Her eyes are pleading now, not just tearing because of her cold. "You always act like you're all alone on everything, Ian, except when you're working on a project with Teddy. But you can get a lot more accomplished if you work together with other people, you know?"

I stand up, unable to face her. I can work with Teddy, but he's the only one. I don't begin to know how to work together with anyone else. "I don't know anything!" I insist.

Luke whispers, *Listen to Sara if you don't want to listen to me, and*—

But I cut him off. *Leave me alone! Just—go away.* And he does.

I turn from Sara's hurt expression and start up the aisle. I have core English and history first period with Mr. Mitchell, and it's on the far side of the school. She's in the same class, but I don't wait for her. For all her journalistic skepticism, Sara trusts other people. I guess that's why she's so big on working together with them. But she doesn't know what they're really like.

rumors

It looks as if nobody's going to make it to class on time. Everybody's just standing around the hallway talking.

"I knew Teddy was trying to find his father," one girl says. She sees me and waves, smiling through warm brown eyes like we're friends, even though I don't know her name. Three elementary schools feed into Sequoia Middle School: Teddy's, mine, and one just north of Sawville. Teddy knows everybody by now, but even though I take pictures of the faces, most of the kids behind them are strangers. "Hey, Ian! Is that right? Did Teddy figure it out and go after him, or what?"

I shake my head. "I don't know." Did the girl really know anything before Mrs. Camden blurted it out, or is she just pretending she'd heard it before, trying to get in on the gossip? If Teddy found out who his father actually was, it's news to me.

"I heard he was getting close," a scrawny seventh-grader says eagerly, not realizing how ridiculous he sounds. He probably barely even knew Teddy. "Wasn't he, Ian?"

"I don't know," I insist, pushing my way through the group.

"I know Teddy was looking for his dad," says Sara, who must have been following me. "And so do you."

"Everybody knows that—now," I retort.

"Well, didn't he say anything to you about finding his dad, or getting in touch with him?" Sara asks, panting a little as she hurries to keep up.

"No," I snap. "Did he tell you that?"

Before Sara can answer, Lynn McKinley smooths her long black hair and looks over at us. As usual, she's part of an animated group. But it's completely unusual for her to say anything to me. "I heard Teddy left to go see his dad, but some stranger abducted him—is that right, Ian?" She sounds almost thrilled at the idea.

"I have no idea!" I tell her, shocked. I can feel them all staring at me, insisting I know, demanding I tell them. Is this the "working together" deal Sara was talking about? Maybe one-on-one some of these guys are all right, but in a group they turn into a hunting pack. How could Sara expect me to work with them on anything?

I'm almost angry at Teddy, too—why didn't he tell me where he was going Monday? His last words yesterday afternoon come into focus in my memory: "I'll be a little late. I've got something I have to do. Then we'll hit the redwoods and snap some shots, okay?" And I can remember his expression, too—he looked really happy. Why didn't he meet me afterward, like he promised?

"Move along, people," a teacher's voice rings out as she brushes past Lynn's group.

I duck my head away from the gossiping kids and retreat into Mr. Mitchell's classroom. But it's no better there. Students cluster in groups, talking, and when I sit down the desk next to me is empty. Teddy should be there.

"Hey, Ian," Craig Leary calls, "what's the scoop on Teddy's father? Did he take Teddy away from that crazy mother of his?"

The kids around Craig laugh. Craig's always the center of his own pack of students, all eager to impress him. If he were one of a hundred kids marooned on a desert island, they'd vote him chief in record time—when Teddy and I watched *Lord of the Flies* on DVD, I saw Craig in Jack right away, gleefully leading the others on a hunt whose horrors they hadn't even suspected yet. He's tall, wire thin and wire taut, with a perpetual sly sneer that transforms itself into an ingratiating smile whenever a teacher turns up.

"Okay, kids." Mr. Mitchell comes into the classroom, his voice strong and clear above the rest. He's short and kind of overweight, and he'd look like a pushover except that when you frame him through a viewfinder you see he's got this strong, square chin and cool blue eyes that size up a student and let him know he's not going to get away with anything. It's strange the way you only see part of people when you look at them face to face. The details don't spring into focus until you look through a camera. I've gotten to the point where I can usually imagine what someone will look like even without the camera, just by watching life through an imaginary viewfinder.

Mr. Mitchell has a reputation as the town eccentric, but I like him. He puts in a lot of time as the publications adviser, and he's always got good things to say about the photos Teddy and I take. But people in Sawville think he's weird because he used to live in San Francisco, even though his family's from here. Most people here haven't ever traveled farther than the mall at Scotia, unless they moved away for good.

Then there's the rumor that he didn't start out as a teacher. Apparently he used to be some sort of psychologist. He certainly makes a big deal about analyzing the psychology of the characters in the books we read. But then a few years ago he quit and came back here to teach. No one has any idea why. Plus he lives all alone on the edge of town in this incredible house that belonged to his family. It's nothing like any other house in Sawville. It looks like something that grew out of the trees and rock slabs leading down to the river below.

"Take your seats, now, and get out *The Moon Is Down*," Mr. Mitchell says, sitting on his desk and swinging one leg. "We've only got the rest of the morning, you know. I'm sure you can waste it if you try, but let's not and say we did, okay?"

Some of the kids laugh, but most don't even hear him. They're still whispering about Teddy.

"Tell me what you think about propaganda and invasion," Mr. Mitchell says as if they're paying attention.

Everybody looks blank for a minute. I've read the Steinbeck book, but nothing comes to mind. It's about the invasion of a little town, written while Hitler was gobbling up Europe. It's a good story, but I hadn't really thought much about propaganda relating to the invasion. Finally Sara raises her hand.

"Well, the invaders try to use propaganda to make the people accept them and work for them," she suggests hesitantly, her stuffed nose making "brabagada" sound funny and unthreatening. Then she digs in her pack for a tissue just in time to catch her next sneeze.

The whispering hasn't stopped. "Good, Sara. Now, does the invaders' propaganda work? You, Craig." Mr. Mitchell points at Craig Leary.

Craig looks up, surprised. Then he grins. "I don't know, Mr. Mitchell. I really can't think about it—I'm so worried about Teddy Camden."

The kids in his group snicker. A few others laugh too, but a lot of them look serious.

"I didn't know you two were such close friends," Mr. Mitchell tells him, cocking one eyebrow and running a hand over his hair. "What about someone else, someone who's not so worry-stricken that his mind is paralyzed in class? or her mind?"

Lynn flips her long hair back over one shoulder and puts her hand up. "It seems to work in the beginning, but that's because the people are confused, isn't it? They never really believe the invaders." She pauses, but Mr. Mitchell lets her finish the thought. Teddy always likes the way he makes us think things through, but sometimes I wish he'd just tell us what we need to understand about a book or a historical event, instead of making us figure it out for ourselves. He's got this poster up in the front of the classroom. There's a silhouetted figure, looking out across space. Words wrapping around the figure read:

> And this I believe: that the free, exploring mind of the individual human is the most valuable thing in the world. And this I would fight for: the freedom of the mind to take any direction it wishes, undirected. And this I must

fight against: any idea, religion, or govern-
ment which limits or destroys the individual.

— John Steinbeck

Mr. Mitchell says if he only teaches us one thing this year, understanding that quote should be that thing. So he makes us think instead of just reading and memorizing.

"Anyway, by the end the propaganda definitely isn't working," Lynn finishes at last.

"No, it's not," says Mr. Mitchell. "And you're right, Lynn—it never really worked. Does anyone have an idea why?"

Sara blows her nose. "Well, the whole point of the book is that free people are slow to react to an invasion, but can't be stopped once they decide to fight back."

Mr. Mitchell nods. "Do you agree?"

Most of the class looks blank. Sara says, "I think—" but then she stops. She shakes her head after a moment. "I'm sorry, Mr. Mitchell, but World War II and Steinbeck just seem kind of unimportant right now. Hitler's propaganda didn't work in the end—we know that. But we don't know what happened to Teddy."

Mr. Mitchell sighs. "Okay—it's pretty clear you can't concentrate on Steinbeck today. So let's talk about Teddy instead." He glances at the window in the door, as if he thinks somebody might be watching, then looks back at us. "But leave your books out on your desks, in case Principal Slater decides to make an unscheduled visit—we all know he doesn't like it when I stray from the curriculum." He winks at me, and I look down, feeling guilty. I know Dad disapproves of Mr. Mitchell, but I don't really understand why. He seems like a good teacher to me.

"So—does anybody know anything about what happened to Teddy Camden?" he asks, and hands shoot up all over the classroom. "Please note I said 'know,'" he points out dryly. "I don't want to hear rumors." The hands slowly fall.

Then Sara raises her hand. "We know he didn't come home last night, right, Ian?"

She had to do it—make everybody look at me and remember I'm the one who ought to know something. I duck my head and nod, wishing she'd kept quiet.

After a minute, Sara says, "We know he's not in school today. And we know his mom's worried about him, and wonders if his disappearing has anything to do with his father."

Mr. Mitchell looks the class over. "That's true—and that's just about all you know, isn't it? Unless somebody has an idea of what Teddy actually did yesterday afternoon?"

He sounds like he's trying to be matter-of-fact, the way he is when he's asking questions about Steinbeck or Hitler's propaganda, but underneath that he also sounds tense—almost as if he's got a personal stake in finding out what happened to Teddy.

Well, Teddy's not just any student to Mr. Mitchell— they know each other from the newspaper and yearbook, as well as the classroom, and Mr. Mitchell likes him. I suddenly find myself looking at Mr. Mitchell through a different viewfinder, and his image shifts imperceptibly from teacher to adult stranger. How old is he, anyway? Old enough to be a parent?

Was Mrs. Camden right? Did Teddy go somewhere with

a man he thought was his father? Could it have been Mr. Mitchell?

When I tried to take his photo for the yearbook, Mr. Mitchell was really hard to shoot. I wanted to get him with the rest of the newspaper and yearbook staff, but somehow the timing never worked out, almost as if he was avoiding me. I finally had to just shoot him in the classroom, barricaded behind his desk. I thought it was going to be a really flat photo, but it turned out surprisingly like him.

No. Suspecting Mr. Mitchell is crazy. I'm so desperate for answers, I'm looking at everyone as if they're hiding something. Mr. Mitchell may have secrets, but that doesn't make him Teddy's father. If it were that simple, Mrs. Camden could have just asked him if he knew where Teddy was.

But I can't help thinking how little we know about anyone. Who knows what Dad's really like behind his public image? Only me, and Mom, because we live with him. And who knows there's anyone beyond the school Ian? Nobody in this classroom, only Teddy. I don't know anything about Mr. Mitchell, except that he has that cool house. Everything else is just rumors.

"Why don't you ask Ian?" Craig demands. "He's Teddy's best friend—he hangs out with him after school every day. If anybody knew what Teddy was up to, Ian would."

Every head in the classroom turns to look at me. Even Mr. Mitchell's. "Were you with Teddy yesterday afternoon, Ian?" he asks, his tone only mildly inquisitive, and I tell myself he's not hiding any secret about Teddy. He's just worried about him—honestly worried, like Sara—not Craig's mock concern or everyone else's thrill of sensationalism. Well, I'm honestly worried too.

I repeat for what feels like the hundredth time, "No, I wasn't with Teddy! I waited for him, but he never showed up. I told Mrs. Camden that already."

The intercom from the office beeps suddenly.

Mr. Mitchell pauses, then turns and calls up, "Yes?"

Dad's voice reverberates through the classroom over the intercom's static, impersonal as if he's talking about a stranger. "Please send Ian Slater to the principal's office. Have him bring his things—this may take some time. The sheriff has arrived to begin his investigation."

The classroom is silent. Then Mr. Mitchell says, "He'll be along in a minute," and writes me a pass.

I can feel the other kids' eyes on me as I start out. Craig says in a low, smiling voice, "Busted."

police interrogation

Mrs. Feeney waves me toward Dad's inner door as soon as I enter the front office. Through the wall of windows behind her I can see the sheriff's two-toned brown pickup parked along the curb, where only school buses are supposed to park.

"Go on, Ian," she says impatiently. "They're waiting for you." She shakes her head. "I just can't imagine what that Camden boy was thinking, running off like that." I guess she'd rather blame Teddy than think something might have happened to him.

I tap softly on Dad's heavy oak door, then open it. A big, balding man wearing a rumpled uniform sits in front of Dad's desk. He's saying in a slow, deep voice, "I very much appreciate your letting us use your office, Mr. Slater. And your assistance in contacting the students' parents for permission to conduct interviews will be a big help."

"I'm more than happy to do anything I can," Dad says, leaning back in his padded leather chair behind his desk. "You may know I'm expecting to move up to superintendent after this academic year, Sheriff—I certainly don't want to leave my old school minus one student." He manages to make it sound deadly serious and like a little joke at the same time.

The sheriff nods and smiles again. "I can understand that, sir." He's holding the family photograph Dad displays on his desk. A slender woman in a skirt and a pale blue blouse sits in the guest chair beside him. There aren't any more chairs.

"Ah, there you are, Ian." Dad's smiling, and the man and woman smile at me too. They don't hear anything but the warmth in his voice, but I know Dad's angry. I just don't know whether he's angry at Teddy for causing all this trouble, or angry at me. Maybe I should have hurried faster. Maybe I never should have been Teddy's friend.

"Get a chair from the outer office and bring it in here, would you?"

I set my backpack on the floor and go outside again. Mrs. Feeney points to a hard wooden chair with curving armrests, and I drag it back into the room. It screeches a little on the polished floor, and Dad frowns briefly. I set it where Dad points and sit down.

"This is my son, Ian," Dad tells the others.

"Hello, Ian," the big man says, smiling faintly at me before turning back to Dad. "You've got a handsome family, Mr. Slater," he says as he replaces the framed photo on Dad's desk.

It's your typical happy family picture—everyone smiling dutifully, Mom in her good dress with a string of pearls around her neck, me in my one suit. No one is touching. I remember once, when I was really little, going in for the annual picture and sort of leaning up against Mom. She put her arm around me, and the photographer smiled. Then

Dad snapped, "Sit up straight, Ian." I sat up straight, and the photographer stopped smiling. He looked at Mom strangely, but she didn't meet his eyes. She just looked into the camera, a polite smile on her heart-shaped face, and her back straight and strong, as if it could bear anything.

In the photo we both look polite, but there's a sad shadow behind our faces. Only Dad's shadow is different. Not sadness—behind that proud smile, he looks lonely somehow, standing ramrod stiff behind the two of us. The picture, just like the one from the year before and the year before that, is so different from the photo I took of Teddy and his mother—her arms flung around him, both of them grinning hugely.

"I'm Sheriff Reynolds, Ian, and this is Deputy Harmon." His slow, deep voice brings me out of the world of the picture and back into Dad's office. I glance up at him and then over at the deputy. She's pretty—soft, dark hair like Sara's.

When I don't say anything, the sheriff turns to Dad. "Perhaps we could have your door closed to give us some privacy while I talk to your son, Mr. Slater?"

Dad calls, "Mrs. Feeney? Will you shut my office door, please? And hold any calls that come in, unless, of course, someone calls with information about Teddy Camden."

After the door closes Sheriff Reynolds turns to me as if we're the only two people in the room. But I can't help seeing Deputy Harmon open her notebook and start writing. And I can't crop my father out of the picture as he sits there, watching me and listening.

"All right, Ian," the sheriff says in his deep voice. "I understand you're Teddy Camden's best friend."

I nod, wondering what conclusions he's going to jump to.

"How long have you been friends?"

I swallow. "Since we started middle school. We both wanted to do photographs for the school newspaper and yearbook."

"I see," he says thoughtfully. "So you two started out rivals?"

He's already putting the pieces together wrong. I shake my head. "No—Teddy said we could do the jobs together. And we always have."

"That's not exactly the way it happened," Dad comments, his tone helpful. "Ian's just being modest. The Camden boy has some talent, but he's not in Ian's league— Ian won the state essay competition last year, did you know that? And when it comes to photography—well, that pack there is full of Ian's equipment. He's already a fine photographer. His pictures of our school athletes have even been in the *Sawville Journal*."

Sheriff Reynolds smiles at Dad's extravagant praise. "Yes, I thought I'd seen Ian's byline in the paper."

As much as I like photographing redwoods, I also like action shots. When you watch a receiver catch a long pass at full speed, or a basketball star sink a three-pointer, all you see is the perfection of the play. But the stills tell the real story behind the action: muscles straining for the ball, drops of sweat on the player's forehead revealing how hard he worked for the play. The local paper doesn't have a full-time photographer, so they buy photos of school games and other stuff from me. Teddy even wrote a macro script for my modem so I can upload from my iBook directly to the computers at the newspaper office.

Sheriff Reynolds is telling Dad, "You're lucky to have a son who's talented and so involved in community activities. Too many boys his age wind up in my office, in trouble."

Then he turns back to me. "So you two split the work?" he asks. "One of you taking pictures for the newspaper, and one for the yearbook?"

I shake my head again. "No, sir. We worked together on both."

"I see." He smiles again. He has a nice smile, in spite of his bushy eyebrows and beefy frame. "A real team effort."

"That's right."

"I hear from Mrs. Camden that you and Teddy spent most afternoons together."

"Yes, sir." I wonder how much to say. Sara would advise me to tell him everything, but I don't know if she's right. I can't even imagine trying to explain my zoning out in a way the sheriff would understand.

I realize he's still waiting to hear about those afternoons. "We take pictures," I tell him. "Sometimes for the paper or yearbook, but most of the time just for practice. We go out in the forest and photograph the redwood trees."

"I see." The sheriff nods. "The redwoods are magnificent, aren't they? It's sad how many kids who grow up here take the forest for granted and can't wait to get out of Sawville."

I nod, thinking I can't wait to get out too, but it's not Sawville I want to escape.

"Have you always taken pictures of the trees?" the sheriff asks.

"I didn't always have a camera," I say, "but I've always

loved the redwoods. Dad used to take me out in the old growth forest when I was little." I can remember him laughing, a big man who could swing me up in the air and over the fallen tree trunks. He'd hold my hand and point out little tree frogs and scurrying chipmunks and bold wrens, and we'd pick up tiny pinecones that held enough seeds to grow hundreds of giant redwoods. He'd tell me, "I always loved the forest when I was a boy—it was my escape. I know you'll love it too." And I did. I do.

Dad smiles suddenly. "My father took me out in the woods when I was growing up," he tells the sheriff. "I wanted to pass them on to Ian, the way he passed them on to me."

Sheriff Reynolds turns to him. "Your father would be Professor Nathaniel Slater, wouldn't he?"

Dad nods, and his eyes get a faraway look, like he's seeing someplace other than his office. He used to look that way sometimes when he was showing me a new path through the trees. He said once, "I wish you'd had the chance to know your grandfather, Ian. He knew every inch of this forest, better even than I do. . . . " His voice trailed off, and I started to ask how Grandfather died, because no one had ever told me anything, but Dad went on, "He mapped the forest—the roads and trails, even little paths like this one that animals made and most people never notice." He chuckled a little. "Dad always carried a sketchbook, to draw the places we explored." Then his smile faded and he shook his head. "I wish I still had those sketchbooks."

I wanted to ask what had happened to them. Had Grandmother thrown them away after he died? I'd never known that Grandfather drew maps and sketched. Most of all, I wanted to ask Dad if he thought my love of taking pictures came from Grandfather. Old-style cameras weren't so effective back when Dad was growing up, not like digital cameras today. Had his father loved making pictures in his sketchbooks the way I loved working on images on my laptop?

But I didn't dare open my mouth. We were comfortable together for once. Dad didn't seem disappointed in me at all, and I didn't want to say the wrong thing and break the spell. I just wanted to enjoy being with him. He finally shrugged and said, "I don't need the sketchbooks, of course. He taught me all the trails so I could follow them even without him." Then he looked down at me and patted my shoulder. "And now I'm teaching you. Only, I promise not to leave you alone. You'd just get lost out here." I was grateful he was there to look after me.

"Quite a distinguished heritage, Ian. Your grandfather would be glad to see you following in his footsteps with your photos," Sheriff Reynolds is saying, and I realize with a shock that I almost got lost in the memory. I glance quickly at him and his deputy, but I don't think either of them noticed anything.

"I guess I always wished there was a way to bring the forest home with me," I say quickly, trying to cover my lapse, "so I started trying to take pictures of it."

The sheriff says, "Those big trees are tough to capture on film."

I nod. "That's why Teddy and I work at it so much. We want to get it just right."

"What kind of camera do you use?"

"A digital 6.1 megapixel with an optical and digital zoom and variable focus and exposure modes and presets," I tell him. "I use it with Photoshop on my iBook."

The sheriff laughs. "That sounds like some sort of foreign language! At your age, I thought a 35-millimeter camera with interchangeable lenses was the top of the line."

I can't help grinning, almost forgetting Dad's presence. "But you need a darkroom for that. It's developing the image that makes the difference between an okay photo and a good one. With digital photography, it's a lot easier."

"I can see how it would be," he says. "Did Teddy have a digital camera like yours?"

I nod. "Not identical—we picked different ones, to compare. We saved summer yard-work money and birthday money and allowances to buy them."

"Sounds like real dedication. Do you want to be a professional photographer, Ian?"

I wish he hadn't asked that. No one except Teddy knows that's my dream, although Sara may have guessed. "I'm probably not good enough," I hedge. "Teddy's the artist with a camera."

I see Dad frown behind the two officers, wanting me to be the best, and I look down, ashamed. I wish I could be the son he wants—the son he deserves. After a moment, the sheriff asks, "So—were the two of you taking pictures together yesterday afternoon?"

And suddenly we're back to Teddy's disappearance. I realize I've relaxed, which was what he wanted me to do—he was only pretending to be interested in my photos so he could manipulate me into talking. I have to be more careful with him. Maybe he's only trying to do his job—but maybe he's the last person I should trust with any information I might know or remember about Teddy or Cal. "No. Teddy said he had something to do, and he'd meet me later, but he never did."

The sheriff studies me thoughtfully. "Did he tell you what he had to do?"

I shake my head. "I wish he had. I wish he'd let me go with him."

"Did Teddy usually go off alone?"

"No," I say helplessly. "We usually stayed together." I feel Dad's eyes on me and know he's thinking I should never have started hanging out with Teddy. I should have come straight home every day, so I'd be there when he arrived, not out in the forest with anyone else.

"So yesterday was very unusual?" Sheriff Reynolds asks, relentless.

I nod. I remember watching the movie of A *Separate Peace* in English last year. It ended in this mock trial where Brinker wouldn't quit grilling Gene. Right now I feel just like Gene. Brinker pretended he only wanted to help Finny accept the truth, but he was really trying to expose Gene's guilt. Is that what the sheriff thinks? That I'm responsible for what happened to Teddy? Is that what he's trying to manipulate me into confessing?

"Did Teddy say anything about when he'd see you next?" the sheriff presses. "You know, 'I'll see you in school tomorrow' or 'I'll call you later tonight' or anything like that?"

"He just said he'd meet me later, and we'd shoot some redwoods," I tell him, more concerned with figuring out what he suspects than with my answer.

"Where was he going to meet you?"

Just like that, it slips out. "At the hideout." And it's too late to call the words back, to say something else—to keep the hideout safe. Teddy's hideout. He's going to be furious I told.

Is this what you call people working together, Sara? Is this the person you wanted me to talk to? Well, forget it! If you trust people, even a little, they don't work with you— they just use you to get what they want! I can't let that happen again.

Deputy Harmon looks up from her notebook. Dad is staring at me. Did I zone out, or are they just shocked about the hideout? Well, that's the last thing they'll get out of me. I don't trust any of them to find out what happened to Teddy. They don't care about him—they just care about solving cases to make themselves look good.

Then it hits me—I'm the one who should find Teddy. He's my friend, not theirs. I'm the one who cares about him.

Sheriff Reynolds says, his voice mild, "Boys always have someplace, don't they? A clubhouse, a campsite—a hideout. Could Teddy have gone to meet you there, Ian? But you'd already left?"

I shake my head, stomach churning as I realize just how much I do want to be the one to find him—not just stand on the sidelines taking pictures for once, but be the one in the middle of the action. The idea thrills me at the same time it terrifies me. How would I start? Not by answering the sheriff's questions, that's for sure. No, I'd start with my dream in the redwoods.

"Did you wait for him?"

I nod, wishing I could answer all the questions like this, without words.

"How long did you wait?"

No gesture I can use for that one. "Until around 5:30. Supper's at 6:00, and I didn't want to be late."

He nods. "Did you say anything to your parents about Teddy not showing up?"

I shake my head, staring at the floor, not volunteering anything. But he doesn't leave it at that. "Why not? Weren't you worried about Teddy?"

I look up. "Of course I was worried! But—" My voice trails off. I certainly won't tell him that Dad wishes I had different friends than Teddy, so we don't talk about him at home.

Sheriff Reynolds just says, "Boys like to keep their secrets, especially when they think their family might disapprove. Maybe Teddy doesn't say a whole lot more to his mother than you say to your parents. What do you think, Ian?"

I blink, not certain what would be a safe answer. Deputy Harmon looks up from her notebook, waiting for me. "I—I don't know what Teddy told his mom. I mean—she knew about us being friends, and spending time together shooting pictures of the redwoods. She's got his photos up all over the house."

The sheriff smiles. "Yes, I saw them. Really good shots." He studies me for a moment. "Okay, then, Ian—here's something you do know that could help us. Suppose you tell us where that hideout of yours is."

Just like Craig Leary said—I'm busted. I try to stall. "We just wanted someplace we could go and mess around with our cameras, you know, downloading the images, and sharpening them and adjusting the color and filters in Photoshop."

"Sure," he says easily. "In my time, you'd have wanted someplace you could turn into a darkroom. Now you just need someplace quiet, I take it?"

I nod, thinking that we really needed someplace where no one would tell us our photos were lousy and we were wasting our time. All I say, though, is, "That's right."

"So—where did you go?"

Finally I admit, "Teddy's mother's family used to own this motel, back when lots of tourists came into town to look at the redwoods."

"Now they stay at chain hotels on the interstate," Sheriff Reynolds says, sighing.

Teddy told me that the motel had been losing money, so they finally closed it. His mother inherited it, but she couldn't pay the taxes or something, so it's been all shut up for years. But the sheriff can find out that stuff from Mrs. Camden, not me. "Yeah, well, Teddy had a key to one of the cabins, and we used it for our hideout." I add, quickly, "We didn't mess anything up or break anything. If anyone ever decided to open the place, we'd just clear our stuff out, and no one would ever know we'd been there."

"I'm sure you didn't damage anything. Where is this place, Ian?"

Now that I've said this much, the sheriff could find it himself. Why is he making me tell him? He probably wants to make sure I get the point that he's in charge. I get it, all right. "Redwood Reststop, it was called. It's just south of town."

He's already nodding. "I've driven by the place plenty of times. It certainly looks shut up from the outside. Which cabin did you use?"

"Number 17, in the back."

He frowns for a moment. "Surely the electricity isn't still running. What did you boys use for your laptop and cameras?"

"Batteries," I tell him, wondering if he's pretending not to know much about computers so I'll let down my guard again. It won't work this time. "You can run for hours before you have to switch. We charge them at home, and then we're set for the day."

Sheriff Reynolds chuckles. "Of course. Modern technology at its best." Then he gets serious again. "Ian, do you think Teddy could be hiding out at the motel instead of going home, for some reason?"

I shake my head. "I guess he could—but I can't imagine him doing it. Why would he?"

He doesn't answer. "If something terrible happened, and Teddy was hurt, say—do you have any idea where he'd go?"

I think again of Cal, but the sheriff is the last person I'd tell about him. I'll start by trying to find him myself, even if I'm not sure he'll talk to me the way he talks to Teddy. I realize I've come up with a plan of action. It feels strange—but good.

All I tell the sheriff is, "I don't know. Maybe he'd go to the hideout, but if he needed help he'd know he wouldn't get any for a while, because I'd be in school today. I guess he'd try to get a message to me, or something."

The sheriff is already nodding, unaware of my plan.

"Just what I thought, Ian. So—have you gotten a message from Teddy?"

I shake my head again, firmly. "No, sir."

"You're sure?" Sheriff Reynolds probes.

I think of Teddy's camera appearing in my backpack. Could he have left a message for me in his photos? I can't wait to download the pictures.

Deputy Harmon looks up again, gently tapping her pen on the notebook while she waits. So I give them an answer that's not a complete lie. "I haven't heard anything from Teddy. I wish I had." I don't dare look at Dad. If anyone in the room can guess that I'm stretching the truth, it would be him. I look at the sheriff, instead. "I hope you find him soon."

That's true—as far as it goes. If he finds Teddy, that would be great. But I don't think he can. I don't trust him, even if he is a sheriff. Titles don't mean much in the end. After all, Dad's a principal. Cal's a nobody, but Teddy trusts him, and I guess I've ended up trusting him also. I'm a nobody too, but for once I think I can make my plan work and do something right for someone who matters to me, when it really counts.

Dad doesn't say anything, and the sheriff just studies me for a few moments, his bushy brown eyebrows drawn together as if he's wondering whether I'm lying. I sit there, trying to look sincere, while my mind races to work out where I'd be most likely to find Cal this afternoon.

Finally the sheriff says, "Okay, Ian, I appreciate your help. And if you do think of anything, anything at all that might help us find Teddy, please get in touch with me right away." He hands me his card. "You can call me at home or at the office, or e-mail me." So he does know more about computers than he was pretending. "If I'm not in the office, someone checks my incoming e-mail regularly." Then he pauses. "I'll have to ask you not to go back to your hideout for a while, I'm afraid. We'll need to check it over."

That takes me by surprise. "But—what about the photography magazines and software manuals and stuff?"

He gives me that deceptively friendly smile again. "Don't worry, you'll get all your stuff back when we're finished. But we need to look through everything carefully, in case Teddy left any sort of clue about what he had planned for yesterday."

A new idea explodes like a flash going off in my brain. I know another place Teddy might have left a clue: his journal! We swore to keep our journals private, but Teddy will understand if I look at his, especially if I discover something that helps me find him. No way I'll trust the sheriff with it, though. So I just nod and say, "Okay."

"You can go now," the sheriff tells me.

I look up at Dad, and he nods. "Leave the chair, Ian. The sheriff will need to speak with some other students." He uses that friendly tone that has won over the rest of the school. Sometimes I wonder why they can't see the edge behind the image. Maybe it's because his friendly, easygoing image is real here—he doesn't care about the students or teachers, only about getting his job done, so he doesn't have to be hard on them. He cares about me and Mom. He loves us, and it really matters to him that we should be perfect, so he can't afford to take it easy on us.

That's when I realize it's not just for Teddy's sake that I hope my plan will work. I want to do something that will make Dad genuinely proud of me for once. He's always said my job was to go to school and get good grades and keep out of trouble and make him proud. I don't get into trouble and I try hard in class, but I know my grades aren't really good enough. That's why winning the essay contest was so important to him—he wanted other people to see that his son could achieve something, and congratulate him for being such a good father.

That's why the one thing he likes about my photos is the way the *Journal* prints them, because then people see them and praise Dad for raising a son like me, the way the sheriff did earlier. If I actually found Teddy myself, the newspaper article would be about me. That would be even better than my byline under a photograph—that would be a real accomplishment Dad could be proud of.

I pick up my backpack and turn to go, eager to get started.

"Oh—one last question."

I turn back reluctantly, and the sheriff asks, "What did you do yesterday afternoon, Ian?"

"I told you—I waited for Teddy at our hideout."

"All afternoon?" he asks, his voice blandly curious. "That was a long time. Didn't you go outside and take any pictures?"

I swallow and tell myself he can't read my mind. Even Dad can't read my mind all the time, 100 percent accurately, and he's had a lot more practice than Sheriff Reynolds. There's no way he can know about my zoning out for part of the afternoon, unless I let it slip, like the hideout. "No—I just sat in the motel cabin, reading a magazine article about new digital imaging software."

"It must have been very absorbing," he says dryly. "So—where did you get that bruise on your face?"

I see Dad frown, and resist the urge to rub the sore spot. "I don't remember," I tell him, struggling to keep my voice even. "Maybe I biked into a low-hanging branch. It happens all the time."

"Does it?" He considers the idea, then stands abruptly, much taller than me, even stooping a little, like a lazy grizzly. He reaches for my backpack. "Let's see your camera."

I hand the pack to him automatically, then say quickly, "The camera's empty, Sheriff. But you can't open its memory without my password."

He raises one eyebrow. "Password?"

I nod. "My iBook and camera both are password protected." That had been Teddy's idea. I never would have thought of it.

The sheriff smiles. "Good thinking. Suppose you set up your laptop and plug in your camera for me, all right?"

I set my backpack down on the chair and unzip it reluctantly. I slide out my shimmering white and silver iBook, attach my camera, and turn everything on. The sheriff watches the screen closely as the operating system loads. Then the desktop picture appears, a photo of a redwood, hundreds of years old and at least sixteen feet in diameter at the base, ravaged by fire and struck by lightning, torn open so you can even walk inside the trunk like a huge cave—but still alive and growing. I took the photo, and it always makes me feel a little better about surviving.

I type in the passwords, not trying to shield my typing from his watchful eyes. I can always change them later. "It takes a few minutes," I explain.

"What's it doing?" Sheriff Reynolds asks.

"Starting up, then searching for the camera's contents." I turn the iBook so he can see the screen more clearly. "See? 'Contents: empty.'"

He scrutinizes the dialog box suspiciously. The moment stretches, and I can tell he's waiting, hoping I'll think he's seen something or guessed something, hoping I'll blurt out an answer to a question he hasn't asked, the way I did about the hideout. But I won't let him catch me that way again.

In the end he only says, "Thanks for showing me. You'd better get to class."

I shut everything down, load the gear back into my pack, and turn once more to go.

"Ian," Sheriff Reynolds says behind me, unexpectedly, "remember—if you think of anything, please give me a call."

I look over my shoulder and nod. "Yes, sir."

Well, I'll remember he said that, so it's not a complete lie.

searching

I feel exhausted, as if I've hiked up the steepest ridge in the forest, but also thrilled to reach the summit. Okay—the sheriff made me tell him about the hideout. That's all I told him, though. He has no idea about my plan. I missed lunch, but I'm not hungry, and I can't even think about core science and math. Nothing matters except looking for Teddy—not class work, or the memory of my dream, or the too-real dread of what might have happened to him. I force myself to concentrate on doing something instead of giving in to grief or fear.

I hide in the boys' bathroom nearest the office, the only one I can count on to be empty, since no one wants to hang out too close to the principal. I just sit in one of the locked stalls for a while, trying to work out the plan's details so I don't screw everything up. The main thing is to find Cal, but if he doesn't want to be found that's going to be tough. What else do I have to go on? Teddy's journals, but they're going to be hard to get, and his camera.

I decide to start with the camera. The hallway by the lockers is still deserted, so I pull out Teddy's camera and shove it into my backpack beside my own. Then I head to the room Mr. Mitchell uses as the publications office.

Electives are last period, and neither Sara not Mr. Mitchell are there yet, but I let myself in with the key that Teddy and I copied last year.

Why would Teddy put his camera in my backpack? And when? Did he put it there on his way to—what? Meeting someone? But if the meeting was important, he would have wanted to take a picture.

He's not the one who put it there, Luke says.

I almost jump. I told him to go away, but he's come back.

I left it for you.

No! It's one thing for Luke to talk to me, but he can't just take off and do things. The very idea is terrifying. *That's impossible*, I try to tell him.

I told you—what happened to Teddy has changed everything.

Stop it! I don't want you here!

I know, and he sounds regretful. *But you've got me. If you'll only listen—*

I won't. You're not even real! Just—get out of my head!

I wait, half afraid he'll refuse to leave, but I hear only silence. That's all I should be hearing, right? Only crazy people hear voices. I put new batteries in Teddy's camera and attach it to my iBook with shaking hands. I have to help Teddy. I have to make Dad proud of me. I can't listen to Luke—I can't be crazy.

I change my access password, then launch the photo program. I type in Teddy's camera password, and his macro script shows the camera contents as empty. It's the same script as the one in my camera—the one that faked out the sheriff. Some things still work like normal, and I tell myself to forget about Luke.

Teddy understands that I want to keep my photos safe,

even without me explaining why. He set up a locked, invisible folder for them and wrote a macro script to run automatically when a camera is connected, so the computer puts up a screen shot of an empty camera. Whether or not the camera actually contains any images, it looks empty. That's what Dad gets when he insists on seeing how I've wasted my time. I tell him I've already erased the photos, and he doesn't know much about computers, so he accepts what he sees. When I actually want to work with the pictures, I type in an extra key combination to open the camera's memory for real.

Teddy loves trying out new macros and hacks. He's even got a program that lets me make phone calls while I'm online—I just need a microphone. He says you can do anything with a good modem—or you'll be able to soon. I can't follow all the programs he's downloaded and hacked into to modify, but I get a kick out of watching his fingers fly over my keyboard, making my iBook do even more than the guys who designed it thought it could do.

I type in the key combination to open the camera's memory, but the screen still reads, "Contents: empty." I must have typed it in wrong. But when I try again, hitting the keys carefully this time, the screen insists Teddy's camera really is empty.

I stare at the blinking cursor. Were the batteries dead long enough to erase the photos? But the backup battery is supposed to prevent that. Didn't Teddy take any pictures at all? Then why did he leave the camera for me? Or did someone else leave it there? Who? (Surely not Luke.) And why?

Before I can try to work through the puzzles, I hear footsteps in the hall, coming closer. I unplug the camera and shove it into my backpack as the door opens and Sara comes in. She must be cutting class too. I hit restart before she can see the screen.

"What's up?" Sara asks. She still sounds stuffed, and not particularly interested.

"Just checking the iBook after the sheriff looked at it," I say, as it chimes and the system reloads.

She watches the desktop picture of the redwood appear, then hauls herself up to sit on top of the worktable and blows her nose. "I think that sheriff's good—he explained what was going on to my mom over the speakerphone without worrying her, so she'd say it was okay for him to talk to me. Then he asked lots of questions, and he really listened to the answers. He'll be able to find Teddy. I'm sure of it."

He certainly asked a lot of questions. And he acts like he's trying to find Teddy, but he's putting the pieces together all wrong.

Abruptly Sara looks up at me. "Oh, Ian—if the sheriff is here, that means this is really serious, isn't it? I mean—I was worried about Teddy before, but I was mostly mad at him for just going off somewhere, and mad at you too, I guess, because you probably knew what he was up to and just weren't telling. You guys always know everything about each other."

She sounds honestly upset about Teddy, and a little resentful of me. She must like him a lot. Even though Teddy isn't here now, I suddenly feel left out. Nobody's ever liked me that much, not since Luke and I were friends, back when I was little—unless you count Teddy himself. Certainly no girl ever has, or probably ever will.

"I'm sorry I practically accused you of knowing something and not telling," she says.

I shrug. "That's okay."

"What did Sheriff Reynolds ask you?"

I tell her he wanted to know what Teddy and I did together in the afternoons and where we hung out, and especially about yesterday.

She blows her nose again. "That's what he asked me too, about yesterday afternoon. I told him Teddy was in here talking to me—bubbling over. Well, you know—he must have been the same with you."

I nod, but I don't know what she means. I can't remember him bubbling over. I mean, I remember other times when he got this excitement high from a great picture or a new hack, but he wasn't like that yesterday.

Was he?

"I was sort of mad at him," she admits, reluctantly. "He was way behind on the yearbook photos, and I was getting worried."

That surprises me. Teddy always meets his deadlines. I'm the one who struggles to catch up. How much else don't I know about him?

"He told me he'd been having some family problems, and he was really sorry that he'd let it get in the way of the yearbook pictures. I wasn't very nice at first," she says sheepishly. "I told him he had enough time to take pictures of trees, so why didn't he have enough time for the yearbook pictures?" She pauses. "The sheriff wanted to know if Teddy told me where he was going. He didn't, of course. If he'd told anyone, he'd have told you."

I wish he had.

"I just told him that Teddy said things were going to be better now that he'd found his father. He couldn't wait to talk to him and get things sorted out."

I shut down my iBook numbly, rocked by this bomb-shell. Teddy hadn't said anything to me about actually find-ing his father, had he? I know the kids were all talking about it today, but that was after Mrs. Camden put the idea in their heads. That's not the same thing as Teddy telling Sara before he disappeared. How could he have told her, and not told me?

Sara goes on, "But I thought he wanted to keep it pri-vate, didn't you? I wonder why your father let Mrs. Camden come to school and tell everyone about it like that." She wipes her reddened nose again, then pitches the tissue into the corner wastebasket. "It was kind of mean. He must have known how—well, upset she was, and that the kids would laugh at her."

I want to tell her it probably never occurred to him be-cause nobody laughs at him, but I can't. *Just open your mouth and let the words out*, Luke suggests, but it's not that simple. I put my iBook away in my backpack, and this time he falls silent without arguing the point.

"Hey—you're not taking off early, are you?" she asks, fi-nally noticing what I'm doing.

I wish I could tell her about my plan, but what if she told me I was crazy to try to find him myself? Even worse—what if she told the sheriff? or Dad? "I just can't stand going to Mrs. Harley's class."

She smiles sympathetically. "You're lucky your dad lets you get away with cutting. I'd get detention, then my par-ents would murder me."

He won't let me get away with it, of course. And her parents wouldn't really murder her.

"See you later," I tell her. Then I get out of the room before she can ask anything else. Hopefully Mrs. Harley will think I'm part of the investigation or something. And maybe Sara can convince Mr. Mitchell not to report me for disappearing during electives. It's just that I need time to think about the period when I zoned out. I need to talk to Cal.

I shut Teddy's camera safely back in the locker, along with the books I won't need for homework I don't know about. Then I slip out a side entrance near the bike rack. In seconds I'm pedaling, wondering where Cal would be. I take a back route through the forest to avoid passing the hideout, since I'm sure the sheriff's people are there by now. They'd notice me biking past, especially when kids are still supposed to be in school.

When I get into the section of the old forest where Cal hangs out, I climb off and walk the bike through the bracken. I can hear dripping fog, so loud sometimes it almost sounds like distant rain. Luke's there again.

See the way the new fronds of fern uncoil from the main stalks? he asks. *They look like fuzzy snails.*

That's the Luke I remember from so long ago, back when I was just a kid. He was a real friend then, not someone always pushing me around. I almost feel little again.

Look. Those bushes will burst with rhododendrons soon.

I run one hand through the thimbleberry bushes, feeling their papery soft leaves and the soft white buds that will burst into flower soon. Shafts of sunlight stream down through mist, lighting the massive tree trunks, and I frame pictures in my mind. But there doesn't seem to be any point in taking out my camera and shooting anything. Not without Teddy.

I wish he'd just materialize out of the forest haze and join us, maybe looking a little tired, maybe kind of disappointed that his father didn't turn out to be what he had expected. Now that I think about it, I'd never fully realized how determined Teddy was to find his father. He'd talked about it for so long, I never noticed when he started actually doing something about it. I wish I'd seen. If I had, I could have warned him that fathers can be hard to live up to.

It's not the same with moms. You play with your mom sometimes, and other times you have to take care of her—but Teddy knows plenty about mothers, even more than I do, probably, because he hasn't had a father to distract him. I could have warned him it can be tough to do everything a father expects you to be able to do. It can be hard, almost impossible, even, to remember that he was a kid like you once, exploring the old forest—hard to imagine what he was like then, when you only know him now.

It seems like Teddy and I talked all the time, but I'm only just discovering how many things each of us left unsaid. Maybe I should have talked more to Sara today.

Yes, Luke agrees, too quickly. *You should have. You have to start sometime.*

I'm trying to start with Cal, if I can only find him.

I remember the first time Teddy and I actually met Cal. People knew about him in town, of course—the weirdo who just turned up one day and seemed to disappear into the redwoods at will. Teddy and I caught sight of him in the distance a few times—swathed in a shapeless, shabby coat that dragged in the duff, with a graying beard, and long, scraggly hair tied back in a ponytail. Sometimes he lugged a bulging, threadbare backpack, and I wondered what was inside. He always struck me as kind of a character out of an adventure movie—like Ben Gunn, skulking around Treasure Island. I'd have just left him alone, but Teddy was curious, so we followed him one day only to find out he'd been watching us too.

"A regular conspiracy of spies," he announced, cackling. I could see dark green woolly patches of stretched-out sweater where his faded coat hung open. "Guess we caught each other at last. So what's it going to be—you here to turn me in? Midnight lynch mob or local firing squad at dawn?"

I wanted to turn and run, but Teddy just laughed. "Why would we turn you in? What's your name, anyway?"

The man just stood there and looked Teddy up and down. I'd have said he looked dangerous, except for the fact he had unexpectedly blue-green eyes that caught the forest light and crinkled at the corners as if dancing with laughter. Up close he seemed almost friendly—more like Long John Silver than old Ben Gunn. "How about if you just call me Cal Samuels." His tone dared Teddy to disbelieve him.

Teddy cocked his head to one side. "Hmm . . . Cal—short for—what? Calvin, maybe?"

Cal shook his head. "Get your mind out of the comic strips, boy, and think closer to home."

Teddy looked perplexed, then grinned. "Close to home? How about California? As in 'California, Here I Come'?"

Cal blinked. Then he laughed. "Clever spy—you've found me out."

"Now what about Samuels?" Teddy wondered aloud. "Cal's short for California. . . . Maybe Sam's short for Sam? Uncle Sam?" He frowned. "But what does that have to do with California?"

With a mock sigh, Cal crossed his arms over his chest and glanced from Teddy to me. "Maybe not such clever spies. Oh well, I guess most folks can't see the real person behind the name. You're just a couple of kids—nothing wrong with you playing at being spies, kind of like making up your own Tom Sawyer and Huck Finn story."

Teddy looked insulted, then thought for a moment. Then he chuckled. "Oh, I get it! Mark Twain wrote about Tom and Huck—and the real person behind the name was Samuel Clemens! That's it, isn't it? Samuels for the real writer behind Mark Twain. But what does California have to do with Mark Twain?" He turned to me, eyebrows raised, but I had no idea.

He worked his way through the question out loud. "Well, Twain sent Huck down the Mississippi to find freedom, and he let Tom keep running away from his aunt." He looked up, his puzzlement fading. "Did you do the same thing? Sure—I bet you did. I deduce you lit out to California like Tom and Huck lit out to find freedom."

Cal did an exaggerated double take. "I take it back, boy. You're better than a spy—you must be Sherlock Holmes!" He jerked one thumb at me, the dirty fingernail poking through a frayed glove. "Complete with Dr. Watson."

Teddy bowed modestly. "So—why did your quest for freedom bring you here?"

Cal's smile faded. "Maybe running from woman trouble," he suggested. Then those blue-green eyes suddenly slid away from Teddy to focus on me. "Maybe running from family trouble." His eyes released me and he looked up innocently at the skies. "Maybe running from the law, or tax troubles, or bill collectors."

"Maybe running from something else altogether," Teddy retorted. Then he dropped the playacting. "So— how can we help, Mr. Samuels?" That's Teddy—always trying to take charge and help someone.

The greenish-blue eyes dropped from the sky and looked at him almost kindly. "You can't, Sherlock." Then he adds, "Well, you can call me Cal."

Teddy grinned. "I'm Teddy Camden, and this—" Don't tell him our real names, I wanted to shout, but it was already too late. "—is Ian Slater. But you can call us Sherlock and Watson, if you'd rather. Anyway—there's got to be something useful we could do."

"I'm sure there is, Sherlock," Cal told him. "But I doubt whatever that might be would concern me."

Teddy rolled his eyes. "Come on—how do you get food? How do you stay clean? Healthy?"

Cal laughed, but he looked pleased, and a little touched. "Look around you, Sherlock. I trap food, or find it." Take it, I mentally amended, figuring that's what I'd seen in the bulging knapsack.

Cal went on, "I stay clean enough swimming in the river, or wash my clothes and body both, walking in the rain. I'm all right, but I thank you for caring—and I'll thank you to keep your mouth shut about me, too."

Of course, Teddy promised for us both, and we'd run into Cal every now and then, even showing him our photos, not thinking it might be important one day to tell somebody we knew him. But now I think it might be. I think I might have to break that promise, if Cal knows anything—or, it suddenly occurs to me, if he did anything to Teddy.

word games

He appears in the shadow of a redwood beside the bike ruts, with no warning as usual. "Been wondering when you'd turn up, Watson," he announces. His fingers are at work, deftly poking a dangling thread through a hole in a well-worn blue sweater. I guess it's too warm for his coat today.

Why was he expecting me? It's the middle of the school day, after all, and I never cut class. Was I right in suspecting he knew something? "Teddy wasn't in school today," I explain. "He never came home last night, and his mom's really scared."

Cal studies me, his blue-green eyes cool and not particularly friendly. "What's it got to do with me?"

That surprises me. I thought he liked Teddy enough to care if something happened to him. I blurt out, "Don't you care?" Then I recover. "I mean—I thought maybe he'd go to you if he needed help. I thought maybe you'd know something."

Cal doesn't say anything. He finishes working the thread through and then shoves his hands into his pants pockets.

Teddy's the one who usually does the talking. I never know what to say to Cal, and today I don't feel like messing around with the playful banter he and Teddy are both so good at. "*Do* you know anything?" I can't help it if my voice sounds desperate. When he still won't answer, I add, "You're his friend!"

Cal snorts. "Thought you were his friend, Watson. Guess I was mistaken. No surprise there—I've been mistaken about plenty of things in my time."

"I am his friend," I retort, stung. How can he even joke that I'm not? "That's why I'm here. I've got to find him— I—well, I want to help him. I thought you'd want to help him too."

Cal says, slowly, "Sure, Watson. Friends do anything they can to help each other." He emphasizes the word "friends" oddly. "Course, sometimes friends get tired of each other, or decide that family comes first. Happens all the time. Then one of them moves on and forgets about the other."

Is he trying to tell me that Teddy found his father and decided that he came first, and moved on? But even if he got tired of me and decided family comes first, how could he leave his mother? "Why can't you just say what you mean?" I demand.

"I always say what I mean," Cal returns. "I figure other people get as much as they want to out of it. Course, sometimes that's nothing at all." He shrugs and turns to go.

"So you don't know anything about Teddy? You can't help me?"

He turns at that. "Help—you? I thought you were trying to help your friend, not yourself."

"I meant—help me find Teddy!" Why is he making it so difficult?

"Did you, now? I wonder what this is really about—you, or your friend." He shakes his head and starts to leave again.

Angry, I almost just jump on my bike and take off right then. But I know Teddy wouldn't want anything to happen to Cal, whether Cal cared about him or not. "Cal, be careful! There was a sheriff asking questions at school. He knows about the hideout, and he's going to have people—deputies or something, searching the forest. Watch out they don't find you."

He stops at that. He stands, his back to me, that tangled gray ponytail dangling down over his shabby sweater, for so long I almost leave. Then he asks, his voice so soft I can barely hear him, "Did you tell them where to find me?"

"Of course not!"

He turns at my insulted tone, his expression puzzled. "Why 'of course'?"

How can I explain I thought Teddy might be with him, and I wanted to be the one to find him, not the police? *Just say it exactly like that*, Luke advises. *I think he'd understand.* I guess Luke likes Cal too, the way Teddy did. I wish I could understand him like they do.

I shrug one shoulder, awkwardly. "You're our friend." Well, he's Teddy's friend. "I wouldn't want anything to happen to you, that's all."

"Like what?"

"They'd ask you questions." It seems rude to tell him that the sheriff would probably think shabby derelicts who hide out in the trees were even more suspicious than teenagers. "They're police! They lock people up!"

Cal smiles faintly. "But you thought I knew something, Watson. What if you're right?" His tone turns faintly menacing. "Shouldn't they ask me in order to find out? Shouldn't they lock me up?"

What's he saying? Teddy would know—and he'd know the right words to say to get a clearer answer.

Ask the right questions, and he'll tell you what he means, Luke advises. But I don't have a clue what the right questions are.

"*Do* you know something?" I demand again.

Cal crosses his arms, his hands balled into fists. "You came here because you thought I knew where Sherlock was." Now his voice is challenging. "Did you think I'd done something to him? Hurt him?"

"I—No!" But did I? He stands there, fierce, and I think of him making it on his own out here. He traps animals to eat them—does he kill them with his own hands? He looks strong enough to break a rabbit's neck—or a boy's.

I remember wondering if Mr. Mitchell could be Teddy's father—that was a dumb idea, but what about Cal? Why did he just show up here all of a sudden? Maybe running away from family trouble, he said—what about running into it? Maybe he came here to find out what happened to the woman he'd known fifteen years ago, and to get a look at his son. I think how much he values his freedom—if Teddy told Cal he knew he was his father, and expected him to stay around, would Cal have lashed out before thinking?

Cal takes a step closer toward me. "Maybe you're right, Watson. Maybe I know exactly what happened to

Sherlock. And now you're wondering if I'm responsible—crazy old guy out here in the trees. Looks guilty as sin, wouldn't you say?"

He uncrosses his arms threateningly and I stumble back, realizing how isolated we are out here in the forest.

Sweat trickles down the side of my face as he leans forward. I feel like Jim Hawkins suddenly discovering that Long John Silver is really a dangerous pirate, not his friend at all. "Don't!"

"Will you run tell your sheriff about me now?"

"I—" I don't know why I hesitate. Won't I tell, if I get out of here alive?

Cal stares hard at me for a long time. Then he shakes his head. "I don't get you, Watson. I only know somebody's not telling the whole story here." He turns his back on me. "Go read about Sherlock Holmes at Reichenbach Falls. Maybe it'll give you some ideas about your friend."

"Wait! What do you mean?"

"Or watch the movie, since you're so into pictures. Black-and-white classic. Same story, same ending." Then he's gone. I scrub a sleeve across my face to wipe off the sweat and start breathing normally again.

What did he mean about Sherlock Holmes at Reichenbach Falls? I've seen the old Basil Rathbone movies on DVD, but I don't remember all the stories.

Think, Luke orders.

I'm trying to think, but I feel tied in knots by Cal's hints and threats and—yes, accusations. Looking around as if the trees might give me some answers, I realize the shafts of sunlight have turned golden and the shadows of the bushes and ferns have grown nearly as long as redwood shadows.

It's a quarter past five, and I head home, pedaling hard to get back in time to clean up before supper at 6:00.

I barely notice the sparse traffic on the winding street as I pump the pedals. I lock the bike in the corner beside the side entrance, having learned in fourth grade that if I expected to keep a bike it had better be out of the way and locked against thieves. No one had stolen it, of course. Dad had warned me to put it out of sight and lock it, and I'd promised I would, but then I just left it lying beside the driveway. "You seem to forget your promises," he'd said. "How am I ever going to teach you responsibility?" Finally he slashed the tires, snapped the chain, and took the bike to the dump. "You'd lose it if a thief saw it just lying there and took it," he'd told me. "So you'll lose it now, until you learn to take care of things."

I'd ridden the school bus, or walked, or driven to school early with Dad, on his way to the middle school. The weekend after Dad trashed the bike, he took me to the big mall at Scotia and bought me expensive new white and green running shoes, like some of the fifth graders had. "Your friends will wish they had a pair just like yours," he told me. I made a big deal out of thanking him, but didn't mention I didn't have any friends. I wished he hadn't given me shoes that I had to work at so hard to keep looking new. But I managed it—I proved I was responsible enough to keep white running shoes pristine. When I finally got another bike, I took care to always lock it out of the way.

I try to close the door quietly behind me, but it's no use.

"Ian—where have you been?" His voice is at once apprehensive and angry. "Didn't you realize I'd be concerned about you?"

"Sir?" I swallow, searching for an answer. I can't tell him I thought I might learn something from Cal that could help Teddy. He'd just want to know why I hadn't told the sheriff—one more way for me to disappoint him. "I'm sorry—" I stammer. "I didn't think—it's not six yet, is it? I didn't think I was late for supper," I finish lamely.

"No, you're not late," he says, that troubled frown still on his face. "But it's not just any day, Ian. With the sheriff at school, and everyone worrying about missing boys—didn't you remember my telling you to come straight home after class?"

Did he? He gives me that strange sidelong look, and I feel off-kilter in a tilting world again. He must have, and I just don't remember.

"You didn't stop and think, did you? You were too busy thinking of yourself to care about anybody else."

I look down, unable to justify my actions. Part of me wants to tell Dad about my plan to find Teddy and get written up in the newspaper as a hero, so he'll understand I was trying to make him proud of me. But if I tell him, then he'll ask what I found out. I'll have to admit I couldn't find anything in Teddy's camera and couldn't get anything out of Cal—I'll have to tell him I failed. It's better to stay silent, even at the cost of knowing he doesn't understand.

"You didn't even go to class this afternoon—I had to tell Mrs. Harley you were so upset about Teddy that I'd sent you home." His voice rises. "Where have you been? I'm waiting for an explanation." He raises one hand as if to shake me, or to knock the answer out of me.

"I just went biking—around some of the places Teddy and I go. . . . " The words tumble out. He doesn't have to hit me, and he almost never does—he says he cares about me so much that it hurts him to hit me, as if he's really hitting himself. But over the last few months he's been acting more strung out, and I'm afraid I might make him lose control one day. The pressure of getting this superintendent job has been so hard on him, and I keep making things worse. I don't mean to, but I know I do anyway. "I'm sorry."

Dad's lips narrow as his face tightens. "Looking for Teddy? Your 'friend' always comes first, doesn't he?" He makes the word sound somehow nasty.

"I'm sorry, Dad," I whisper. "I just didn't think."

"You never think," he says heavily. "You never try to make things easier on your mother or me. You just think about yourself."

He's right, of course.

"You have your little hideout," Dad goes on, shaking his head. "What do you need a hideout for, anyway? What do you do there that you have to hide from your family?"

"Nothing—just take digital photos," I stammer. "It's just a place to work on the images—study the manuals—stuff like that."

"And you can't do that at home? You can't be bothered to show me your photos? Who got you the laptop?"

"You did," I say, knowing how expensive it was, knowing he couldn't really afford it on his salary, knowing he got it for me anyway, so he could say he got me the best equipment to shoot photos for the yearbook and newspaper.

"And you repay me by hiding away from me—keeping secrets from me." He lets the words just hang there. He's always said there's nothing Mom or I can't tell him, nothing he can't help us with. He doesn't have friends he runs to, to complain to about us, friends he goes out drinking with or anything like that. We should be thankful he's there for us, and we shouldn't need anyone else.

I've never put anyone first—more important than my family—not even Teddy. And I'm not keeping any big secrets that he'd be shocked to find out about. All I wanted was a place where I could be myself and feel I was good at something. All I wanted was a friend I didn't disappoint all the time.

"Tell me, Ian," Dad says gently.

But there's nothing I can tell. I look at him helplessly, knowing what's coming next.

"Fine," he says, his voice flat, as if I've hurt him so deeply he can hardly bear it. "I'll let you think about it before dinner. Now take off those filthy shoes before you make more work for your mother."

There's no point in arguing. I leave the hiking boots in the side room, then follow him. He opens the door of the storage closet beneath the stairs and gestures me inside. I stoop down and go in. Then he shuts the door and latches it.

"Just think about it, Ian." His disappointed voice is softened by the wooden door, even though his words are inflexible. "I'll expect you to have a good answer for me when I open this door."

I sit hunched in the cramped dark, knowing there's nothing more I can tell him.

the closet

I hear Dad's footsteps recede and feel some of the tension go out of my shoulders. Dad hasn't realized that I've made the closet my friend over the years, that I feel safer in here now than I felt in the hallway with him. He's never discovered that I sleep here sometimes.

Normal closets contain things like coats or vacuum cleaners, but this closet is the place that contains the failure Ian, the one who knows he can never be good enough. The home Ian walks a tightrope trying to measure up to the perfect son Dad deserves, but there's no way he can always succeed. When he fails, he can escape inside the closet.

I used to hate being shut in here when I was little. It seemed like a huge, dark cave back then. The bugs scared me, and the creaks on the stairs above made me jump, and I'd cry until my eyes hurt, so I could barely see when Dad finally let me out. But I finally convinced myself that the failure Ian was safe inside the closet. Here, there's no one I can disappoint.

I vaguely wonder how long I'll have to stay inside this time, but it hardly matters. I have no reason to get out. I don't know if Mrs. Harley assigned math or science homework—but if it isn't done, the worst that can happen is that she'll say something to Dad. He'll be disappointed I've let him down again, but he'll know the reason why. And I've already finished reading *The Moon Is Down* for Mr. Mitchell.

I liked the ending—the mayor stood up to the invaders after all. He did it in a quiet way, because he said he wasn't very brave. But he was braver than anyone realized—he was scared, yet he still refused to tell the freedom fighters to stop, even knowing the invaders were going to shoot him because of it. Teddy liked it when the freedom fighters struck back and started killing the invaders. He'd do that—ambush invaders and fight back—he's that kind of brave. But not everyone can be brave that way. I couldn't. I don't know if I could even be as brave as the mayor, knowing the price for disobeying and doing it anyway.

I close my eyes so there is no dark, only peace. I can almost see the mayor in my imagination. Alone in the closet I escape into worlds of moving images, stories where everything comes out all right. When I was little, I used to watch cartoons in my mind while I was shut in here, playing them again and again. I loved Yogi Bear cartoons—he and BooBoo would get into all sorts of trouble in the forest, but in the end nothing terrible ever happened. Looking back, I can see I was such a baby then, having faith in a couple of cartoon bears. But playing their adventures in my mind's eye made me think that things might work out okay in the end for me, too.

As I got older, I'd watch movies in my mind—adventure movies Teddy and I biked into town to see, or rented to watch at his place, or on my iBook; or movies that Dad took me to see on afternoons when he was pleased with me.

I lean back against uneven boards that feel almost like redwood trees, towering above me. I imagine myself in the forest—alone, quiet, safe on the soft duff. If the floor gets too hard after I've been in here a long time, I start imagining it's a log I'm sitting on, or a tangle of roots. You can sit anywhere, even a hard place, as long as it's peaceful.

In the closet I don't have to pretend to be the perfect son Dad wishes he had, or smart and talented like Teddy and Sara think I am. I can just be the failure Ian, and not disappoint anyone. I lean back and let my mind drift, like a tiny pinecone floating down through the fog. I always loved thinking how my huge redwoods come from those little cones. Time has no meaning any longer, and I'm in a different zone, hidden in the fog, at peace.

I hear the sudden scrape of the bolt, and tense.

"Are you ready for supper?"

I blink in the light that comes through the closet door, silhouetting Dad's bulk.

"I'm sorry I didn't come straight home," I say quickly.

"And do you have any explanation for that hideout of yours?"

"I was just being selfish," I whisper.

He nods, his eyes tired. "All I ask is that you obey me, Ian, and you won't even do that."

"I'll do better," I promise, wishing I could be the obedient son he wants, and wishing I could tell him that. But he wouldn't believe me, because I can say I want to again and again, and it doesn't mean anything unless I can actually be the son he deserves. "I promise."

Dad looks at me steadily for long moments, his face still

shadowed by the hall light. Finally he reaches out to help me crawl out of the closet. "All right then."

I take his hand in silent thanks. When I straighten up, he smiles and cuffs me playfully on the shoulder before latching the door behind us. "I know you'll try harder—you're my son."

I clean up before going to the dinner table, grateful to him for forgiving me, willing myself not to think about Teddy anymore. It's just tuna casserole tonight (I know how expensive food is, which makes it all the worse that Dad spent so much money on my iBook and I waste it taking tree pictures that he despises), but we're sitting in the dining room with the good dishes like we always do.

Before I can stop myself, I remember eating at Teddy's a few times. He and his mom just eat in the kitchen, and if one of them spills something nobody minds. Dad insists we use the white linen tablecloth and the linen napkins his mother gave him for a wedding present. I put Teddy out of my mind and remind myself to be the at-home Ian, careful not to spill anything. If I do, Mom has to soak the linen and bleach it until every trace of the stain comes out.

"That's all?" Dad says as he sits down, and I can hear his voice tighten in disappointment again. But it's not me he's upset with this time.

I slide into the chair, trying to make myself small so I won't attract his attention, and feeling guilty because if I make myself invisible, he'll focus on Mom. She comes in quickly from the kitchen carrying a serving bowl. "Here's the salad, honey," she says softly, as if her voice could soothe him. "I kept the rolls hot in the oven for you. It'll just take me a second to get them, and the green beans."

"You'd think I could sit down at my own table and have my food on time," he tells her. "It's not as if you work all day, Sandra."

Dad expects Mom to uphold her position in the community as his wife, so she's on the Friends of the Library board and does volunteer work, like fundraising for the local National Park Service branch that takes care of this part of the forest. And Dad expects every inch of the house to be spotless. There can't be any dust trapped in the static on the television screen when he switches it on, the first cobweb in the attic, or a shadow of silver tarnish on the tea service that sits unused on the dining room sideboard. His shirts have to be starched and ironed. The sheets have to be changed every day. And no matter how hard she works, he always finds something she's missed: a discolored tile in the corner of the bathroom (the stain so faint I can't see it at all) or a brown leaf on one of the plants in the living room. I've never understood why everything has to look so perfect—but I do it myself, touching up photos to get the perfect image.

Mom doesn't answer back any more than I do. "I know, Chris," she says, hurrying in with the basket of rolls and bowl of beans. "I just wanted everything hot for you."

"Tuna again," he says, shoveling a heap of the casserole onto his plate. "You'd think we could have some decent food."

Mom takes the smallest roll from the basket, then hands it to him. "I'm sorry, honey. I saved to get a pork roast for tomorrow night, when your mother comes." Dad budgets every penny he gives Mom for groceries and stuff, just like he budgets my allowance. But I guess she's no better than I am at deciding how to spend his money on the right things.

I'm careful not to take too much of the casserole, and I eat really slowly and carefully so as not to make any mess. I don't mind not eating much tonight, but I can't help thinking how good Mom's pork roast is, and how little I'll be able to eat tomorrow with Grandmother there.

Dad heaps salad onto his plate. "I've sure come a long way—the only time I get a decent meal is when my mother comes to visit." He passes the bowl my way, not looking at me. "And your friend Suzy Camden tried to make a fool of me today, blabbing to my students about her kid—she was half-drunk, first thing in the morning!"

Mom blinks, confused. "She's not my friend, Chris."

Dad shakes his head, his voice so low she has to lean forward to make out the words. "You don't remember her coming over all the time to visit you when we were first married? I couldn't come home from a long day surrounded by screaming kids without finding her here, stinking the place up with her cigarettes and keeping you from taking care of my house."

Mom hangs her head. "She's not my friend anymore," she says quietly.

"Now her kid is your son's best friend," Dad snaps.

Mom glances at me, a brief shadow of regret crossing her face. Then she reaches up to smooth her thin brown hair, and the expression disappears as she looks back at Dad. "I'm sorry, Chris. Is—is there any news about Teddy yet?"

"No," Dad snaps, banging the bowl of green beans down hard so the glasses shiver. "But I had to waste school time taking care of Suzy's responsibilities because she doesn't care enough to look after her family herself. No wonder her kid wanted to get away from her."

Mom sits there, eating quietly, her expression blank as his words wash over her. I've always wondered if she's got her own way of zoning out, only she does it when he criticizes her, or me, or people she knows. She seems to go to a secret place where she can't hear him, or where words don't mean anything so they can't hurt. If they hurt her, she'd get mad, wouldn't she? She'd yell at him, or cry, or run away—maybe even take me with her. But she doesn't do anything. I wonder if her stomach burns when she eats, the way mine does.

"I hope I didn't make you miss anything important, calling you out of Mitchell's class," Dad says.

My attention snaps back to him, trying to gauge the potential hazards of the question. "Sir? Uh—just a discussion about propaganda and World War II. And a Steinbeck book—*The Moon Is Down*."

Dad snorts. "Surprise, surprise. Trust that sissy Mitchell to miss the point of the war and teach you about some pathetic novel instead. It's no wonder he came running home from San Francisco with his tail between his legs. I only ask myself what I did to get stuck with him in my school!"

I don't ask what he means with that "tail between his legs" comment. I just force down a little salad and try to ignore the stomach pain. It never hurts when I eat at Teddy's house.

Mom goes on raising forkfuls of casserole to her mouth mechanically. She's told me again and again that Dad works hard for us and aspires high for us, and so of course he's tired and frustrated when he comes home. "He needs someplace safe where he can vent his feelings," she's said, so often I know it by heart. "It's our job to take it. Some men don't care about their families—some men even leave them. We're lucky that your father is willing to take care of us, and if he criticizes you or me it's because he wants us to live up to his high standards."

I know she's right about me not being able to live up to his standards, and right that I should accept what Dad says about me. I can do that. I just don't understand how he can say the same sort of things about Mrs. Camden and Mr. Mitchell. Well, I guess I understand how he can criticize Teddy's mom, but Mr. Mitchell? He doesn't seem like a sissy to me.

But Mom is right that some men don't care enough about their families to stay with them—Teddy's father walking out on his family is what got us into this mess. I try to imagine what Mom and I would do without Dad, and the thought feels like a pit gouged out of our lives. No matter how hard it is to live up to his standards, I know we're lucky Dad's here to take care of us.

The meal drags on until Dad has cleaned his plate and Mom jumps up to take it for him.

He glances at me. "Help your mother, Ian."

I slide off the chair and carefully carry plates and silverware into the kitchen. When I set them down and start back for more, Mom touches my arm lightly, just for a second.

"I'm sorry about your friend."

I look up at her, surprised. Mom and I don't talk to each other much anymore. When I was little, before I started school, she would laugh and play games with me during the day, before Dad came home. We'd rent videos, and giggle at old animated movies, and sing along with them. But now it seems we're hardly ever alone together in the house without him.

"What are you two conspiring about in there?" Dad calls. It could almost sound like a joke, but we both know it isn't. That's why we don't talk much.

Mom's already gone blank as she heads back into the dining room, and I follow her. "I'm sorry, Dad," I say as I pick up the salt and pepper shakers and the butter plate. "I was just asking Mom where to put the leftovers."

He studies me through narrowed eyes, then flicks one hand at me, and I hurry back into the kitchen. Mom doesn't even smile when we pass this time.

As I pick up the last of the supper dishes, Dad says, "Help your mother bring in dessert, now."

"Yes, sir," I say, surprised. Unless Dad specifically invites me to stay and have dessert, I never expect any. It's the one part of the meal where Mom manages to stretch her budget enough to splurge. I don't know why he's letting me have some tonight. It's cheesecake covered with chocolate sauce, so rich I can barely swallow it. Dad takes huge bites, savoring them. He smiles at Mom, finally, and she smiles back as if she's already forgotten his early criticism.

"This is good," he says, his voice deep with approval, and she almost blushes.

It's a relief to go upstairs to the room where I sleep.

Your room, Luke surprises me by practically shouting. *Say it: your room!*

But it's not my room. This is Dad's house, and every room in it is his. I'm not even allowed to close the door.

Dad says that closed doors hide secrets.

I set my backpack down on the empty desk. Without homework, there's nothing to do up here—just charge my iBook and camera batteries, and wait for tomorrow. The backpack and camera and laptop are mine, even if nothing else is. I look at the room around me. Luke's wrong. It's not really my room, any more than it was ever his, even back when he was with me most of the time. But Luke usually came out in the forest, not the house. Except for the desk, a chair, a small chest of drawers and a twin bed, the room around me is empty—no toys, or games, or books that aren't for school, no sports balls or bats—nothing to show that a kid grew up here. I'm supposed to keep the room clean and neat. That means nothing Dad doesn't think I need.

When I was a baby, Dad was determined to prove how smart I was. He bought me these educational toys to give me a head start. I don't remember most of them, because I couldn't make them work and Luke thought they were silly, but suddenly I recall one I haven't thought of in years— this little camera made of bright red and blue and yellow plastic. It even made a clicking sound when I pushed a button, like I was actually taking a picture. I loved that camera. I kept the viewfinder glued to my eye, clicking away like crazy.

Dad realized pretty fast that the educational toys were wasted on me. "I was so proud when I found out I was going to have a son," he told me. I can still hear his voice echoing in the room. "And look what I ended up with." What was he hoping for, anyway? A boy who would explore the redwoods with him? But he got that, and it's not enough.

When Dad started throwing the toys away, I hid the camera, but he found it in the end. He shut me in the closet to think about why it was so terrible of me to lie to him and keep the camera when he'd thrown out everything else. That was before the failure Ian made the closet into a friend, and I cried so hard my face was swollen and sticky. I finally curled into a corner and squeezed my eyes shut to escape into a cartoon movie world, wishing that Peter Pan would take me away to Never Land, where no one had to struggle to please a father. "Second star to the right," I whispered over and over, "and straight on till morning." But Peter Pan never came to lead me to the other Lost Boys, and Luke didn't know the way.

When Dad let me out, he made me take the camera and smash it on the kitchen floor, again and again, until the plastic shattered into a million bright-colored pieces. I wanted Luke to help, but he'd gone away. Dad made me pick up all the pieces and put them in the trash. Then he patted my head, and even squatted down and wiped off my face with a cool cloth. "There," he said, "you see? I knew you could do it. You're my son, Ian—you can do anything you set your mind to."

I finally force the memory back into the zone where I don't have to think about it. That probably wasn't the way it really happened, anyway. I'm remembering it all wrong. So what if I try to do things? It doesn't count for anything because that's all it is: trying. I tried to find out what Cal knew today, and I'm still convinced he did know something, but I can't work out what he meant. The clue he gave me doesn't make any sense. What ideas could Sherlock Holmes at Reichenbach Falls give me about Teddy?

But that's one thing I don't have to give up on. I start up my iBook and sign online. It only takes a few seconds to find a site with the Sherlock Holmes stories and look up Reichenbach Falls. And there's the answer: Holmes died, struggling with Professor Moriarty at Reichenbach Falls. At least, everyone thought he died—even the author meant for him to be dead. But he survived and came back in disguise in the next story.

Maybe Cal meant that Teddy was okay and would come back like that. But why didn't he just say so? That answer seems clear enough—he doesn't trust me. I just can't see why not.

I climb into bed, drained, and lie in the dark, hugging the pillow as if it could hug back. At some point I must drift into sleep, because I'm dreaming I'm in the redwoods again. I see the same fern-filled grove of trees, shadowy in the fog. Over the running water, I can make out Teddy's voice, even though I can't see him.

"Ian? You know where I am—why won't you come help me? I'd help you."

I twist and turn, pushing feebly at bracken that seems to blanket me. I can't help Dad—I can't help Teddy—I'm useless even in my dreams. "I looked all afternoon. I even found Cal and asked him, but he wouldn't tell me. I don't know where you are. I don't know anything. I can't know anything!"

Then I think of his secret. "But I'll get your stuff tomorrow—I had to tell the sheriff about our hideout, but your journals are safe. I'll put them someplace safe. I promise."

There's nothing for a moment—just a sigh, as if the wind has picked up in the distant treetops. Then Teddy says, "That's not enough. Those are just things—what matters is people. You have to come help me."

"I can't," I cry. "I want to, but I can't do anything except take pictures."

Teddy's voice is relentless. "You can expose the truth!"

"But I don't know what the truth is—how can I do that?"

"You have to show them the truth!" Teddy insists. His voice reverberates through the grove, until the redwoods themselves tremble.

I sit upright in bed, shaking my head, for once not believing Teddy. It was only a dream—he'll turn up today, somehow, safe like Sherlock Holmes, and he'll explain what happened and everything will be okay.

I hug the pillow, trying not to see the grove of trees, soft in the bushes' spring growth, cool and peaceful—except for Teddy's cries and those flashes of blackness every time I look around, like the after-blindness that comes when someone snaps a flash photo without warning.

What did he mean—expose the truth? It's a weird phrase. Then I remember that's how you took pictures before digital cameras. You literally exposed the film to light in order to take the picture. Then you used chemical baths to develop the negative so you could print the photograph. Was Teddy talking about his camera? But there weren't any pictures in it. And anyway, I don't know any truth to expose.

I can tell you, whispers Luke. *It's time—*

No—it's not! I tell him flatly, and his voice dies away, leaving me wishing I could hide in the closet from him as well as Dad. I feel guilty at failing him, but I have a vague, unfocused memory that's burned far back in the zone, a memory of listening to Luke and disappointing Dad bitterly. I decided then that I'd rather lose Luke than betray Dad, and I won't go back on that now. But why has Luke come back, after I made him go away?

I rub my sore cheek, straining to see Teddy through the fog that masks the scene like a distorting filter, but afraid to go back to sleep and dream of him again. Has Luke returned to *make* me help Teddy?

Is he back because what happened to Teddy is my fault? Is it my own guilt I have to expose?

wednesday: propaganda

Finally I hear Dad's car leave and drag myself downstairs. I feel wrung out and fuzzy-headed, as if I never slept at all. I pour some juice and look at the newspaper Dad has left on the spotless kitchen table. The front-page headline clears my head: "Site of Missing Boy's Struggle?"

I set the juice down unsteadily and read the article. The sheriff's deputies found signs of a violent struggle near a place called Fern Grove in the redwood forest. Based on some debris they found in the vicinity and down the slope leading to the river below, they suspect that something happened to Teddy at Fern Grove. They're searching the surrounding undergrowth and dragging the river.

The article doesn't say it in so many words, but I can tell the sheriff thinks he's dead. You don't drag the river for someone who's still alive.

There's a picture. I look at it and sink into one of the kitchen chairs. It's the grove I've been dreaming about.

"You do know the truth!" Teddy insisted in the dream.

Why did I dream of the grove? What do I know?

I want to pray, but I can't believe God would listen to me. We go to church every Sunday—Dad sitting there with

Mom and me on either side of him. I stay silent, head bowed like Mom's, both of us looking as if we're praying when we're really hoping no one will notice us. Just in case they do, of course, it's the committee Mom and the public Ian they would see. God couldn't possibly pay attention to my poor prayers—I don't go to church for His sake, but for Dad's.

All the same, a whispered prayer slips out, only "Please . . . please." Maybe I mean "Please help Teddy," or maybe "Please help me." I'm honestly not sure, any more than I'm sure who I'm praying to, or whether anyone other than Mom upstairs might actually hear me. If there is a God, however, He might answer a prayer for Teddy's sake, even if I'm the one asking it.

And maybe He does, because I find myself staring at the paper with new resolve. Maybe I gave up on Cal too easily yesterday. I've got to find out some real answers, not just dreams. I've got to come up with a new plan—find Cal again, make him talk—get the journals, see what Teddy wrote. I pour the juice into the drain, wash the glass, and go to school. I don't think I could keep any breakfast down.

In homeroom Dad's concerned, caring voice comes over the intercom to announce that the sheriff will be asking certain students to speak with him, as he did yesterday. Also, guidance counselors are available to talk with any kids who are troubled about Teddy Camden's disappearance. All around me, kids' hands shoot up—I guess they figure it's an easy pass out of class. The last thing I want to do is talk to a counselor, in spite of Sara's worried frown as we walk to Mr. Mitchell's class.

"Are you all right, Ian?" Her voice sounds worse than

yesterday, more stuffed, and hoarser. "You look really pale. I think you should talk to somebody."

Of course I'm pale. I'm seeing my best friend's ghost in dreams.

Anyway, I know what Dad would say if I talk to anyone. He always says there's no problem that we can't help each other deal with (he means there's no problem he can't help Mom or me deal with) without an outsider's help. Now he'd say that counselors are for other students, the ones who don't have a father like him to take care of them. So I shake my head. "I just didn't sleep well last night."

She nods, her brown eyes magnified behind those purple glasses. "I know what you mean." No, I think, she doesn't. She doesn't have a ghost begging her to find him.

"I was tossing and turning and thinking all sorts of terrible things about what might have happened to Teddy," she goes on. "But the sheriff is really stepping up the search—I'm sure they'll find him."

Didn't she see the paper this morning? The sheriff's deputies aren't looking for Teddy, lost or hurt, anymore. Now they're looking for a body.

When I don't say anything, she asks, "Why don't you want to talk to a counselor? That's what they're here for."

"I don't think so," I tell her.

She sniffles. "Well, you're not acting like yourself at all."

I'm not? How should I be acting, if I'm going to seem more like the school Ian she thinks she knows?

"You haven't taken any photos all week, have you?"

She's right about that. I haven't. There doesn't seem to be any point to it anymore. Teddy's the one who gave her the good shots, not me. She looks up at me, her face worried, and I can see my own reflection in her glasses—two Ians, both looking wan and hollow. I have to answer somehow, even though there's no answer to give. Finally I say, "I've had other things on my mind than taking pictures."

"You know, there's nothing wrong with letting someone help you!" Sara says, her voice severe. "We all need to ask for help sometimes, just like we should be there to help our friends when they need help." When I don't say anything, she bursts out, "Well, if you can't talk to a counselor, you can talk to me—that's all I'm saying!"

Somehow we've reached the classroom door, and I'm relieved because I can't think of any way to answer her. Mr. Mitchell comes out, smiles at Sara almost perfunctorily, then beckons me to one side of the hall.

"How are you handling things, Ian?" he asks, sounding concerned.

I wish everyone would stop asking questions. I've got all the pressure I can handle. "I just want to know what happened," I tell him shortly.

Mr. Mitchell gestures Sara and the other kids into the classroom. She goes with a last worried look at me before he pulls the door shut, studies me silently, then asks, unexpectedly, "Did you and Teddy have a fight?"

I look at him, confused. "A fight? No—of course not." Teddy and I don't fight.

Mr. Mitchell shakes his head, perplexed. "Well, I wouldn't have thought so, but you're not acting like yourself—showing up with that bruise on your face yesterday as if you'd been fighting, and cutting class yesterday afternoon."

First Sara says I'm not acting like myself, and now Mr. Mitchell. I don't see what's so different about me today. And I can understand them caring about Teddy, but why are they worried about me?

Because you're their friend, as much as Teddy is, Luke tells me. I can't understand why he keeps coming back in spite of my rebuffs. His voice sounds irritated with me for being slow on the uptake. *Friends care about each other. You know that.*

Do I? Well, sure I do—I care about Teddy.

"I think this is tearing you up, Ian," Mr. Mitchell continues. "You need to talk to someone."

He's right, Luke chimes in, *Talk to him—tell him about your dreams, about what you remember, and what you don't.*

"Did you know I used to be a child psychologist? Not that you're a child," he adds, inviting me to smile at the thought, even though I can't. "But I have some experience listening, and talking about tough problems." When I don't say anything, he sighs. "It doesn't have to be me, of course, but the counselors—"

"No!" I feel myself shaking. Everybody wants me to talk to someone, work with someone—everybody except Dad. With Teddy gone, more than ever, the person I need to obey is Dad—not Luke, not Mr. Mitchell. "I don't want to talk about it. Please!"

Mr. Mitchell leans against the wall and puts his hands in his pockets. "I know it can be hard to face up to things. I think you need someone to help you deal with what's happened to Teddy." He looks more concerned than angry. "Look, Ian—I've seen you, well, drifting away in class, as if you're not even listening to what I'm saying."

See? Luke interrupts. *He already knows some of it. Now tell him the rest—or let me tell him!*

Luke sounds so eager. But how can I just tell Mr. Mitchell about him when I don't even understand him myself? I figured out a long time ago that people would think I was crazy if I said anything about Luke. I can't see how making Mr. Mitchell think I'm crazy could do anything to help Teddy.

"Ian? Are you still there?" Mr. Mitchell frowns. "You were drifting again."

I just stare at him, feeling a chill that has nothing to do with the school air-conditioning. Maybe he already thinks I'm crazy.

Then it doesn't matter if you tell him, Luke urges.

Shut up! I'm careful to make sure I don't slip and say the words aloud.

"How about if I give you a pass to talk to one of the counselors now?" he suggests. "You can tell the counselor I made you go if you don't want to ask for help."

I know how disappointed in me Dad would be if a counselor mentioned I'd been in to talk. I have a dim memory of talking to someone else once—I think it was Luke's fault. Maybe that's why I know it's such a stupid idea to do it again. I just mutter, "I don't want to," and start for the classroom.

But Mr. Mitchell shakes his head firmly. "Look, I don't want to have to order you to go," he says, his blue eyes staring sternly into me. "It would be—insulting. But whether you talk to me or talk to a school counselor, you have to talk to someone. You decide whom."

He looks as if he doesn't like me very much at the

moment, but I can't let him send me to the counselor's office, no matter what I have to do.

"I'm not going," I tell him, ignoring the faint unsteadiness in my voice. "Dad would think talking to a counselor is a waste of time—of course, he thinks most of what we do in your class is a waste of time, too."

Mr. Mitchell draws back, crossing his arms almost protectively in front of his chest. I'm not surprised to read disappointment in his eyes. "Do you feel the same way, Ian?" he asks quietly. Of course I don't, but I can't tell him that. I just shrug one shoulder halfheartedly.

Finally he sighs. "I think you're making a mistake, but I won't force you if you absolutely refuse." I just look down at the scuffed floor in silence until he opens the door and waves me inside.

"Oooh—teacher's pet!" sings out Craig Leary. The other kids laugh.

I try to ignore both the heat rising up my neck and Teddy's still-empty desk. I turn my back to it, pull out a notebook, then sit down.

"Okay," Mr. Mitchell says, sitting on the edge of his desk and taking a deep breath as if to switch gears. "Who found out something about the effect *The Moon Is Down* had on people during World War II?"

That must have been the homework I missed. I wonder what effect a book can have. It's just words and ideas—it doesn't change anything, not like *doing* something (like following Teddy on Monday afternoon would have).

Sara says, "It got crummy newspaper reviews." Trust her to check old papers. "The critics said Steinbeck made the villains too human—that Nazis were monsters."

"That's what they said all right," Mr. Mitchell tells us. "And do you agree?"

Craig waves his hand. "About the Nazis? Sure, they were monsters."

"Is doing monstrous things the same as being a monster?" asks Mr. Mitchell. I think it is, but I don't raise my hand.

Lynn shakes her head slowly. "I think it's scary the way the colonel is perfectly polite and civilized, and the mayor even likes him, but the colonel is executing people anyway—it's actually more believable than the super villains in comic books."

I shiver inside, where it doesn't show. Maybe the colonel's public image looks civilized, but his private self can still be a monster.

Mr. Mitchell nods. "Nazis were people first, before they joined the party to defend their homeland, or to satisfy some private inadequacy, or because they were pressured, or for as many reasons as there were people living in Germany. We like to think that people who do bad things are monsters, because it's easier to hate them, but the world is more complex than that."

He sits on the corner of his desk. "Steinbeck wanted to put readers right in the middle of that complexity, even though we weren't involved in the war yet. He wanted people to imagine how it would feel if America were invaded, like the European nations. But government censors were afraid that idea might demoralize Americans. So Steinbeck recast the book in an unnamed foreign country. Can you guess what happened?"

Nobody volunteers. "Every European country that had

been invaded thought it was about them," Mr. Mitchell says. "The Resistance smuggled copies of the book into occupied lands and passed them from hand to hand. A Swiss professor later said it was the most powerful piece of propaganda ever written to help democratic countries resist totalitarian occupation."

I stop taking notes, surprised. Can a book make people act differently in real life? Can it give them courage and hope? I wish I had a book that could do that for me.

You have me, Luke whispers. *If you'd only listen to me.* But it's not the same.

Sara's hand shoots up. "So Steinbeck wrote his own propaganda to make people stand up against the Nazis!"

Mr. Mitchell nods. "Exactly." He stands up. "Now—I want you to write me a piece of propaganda. You could write a parable, like *The Moon Is Down*, or a speech that someone like a head of state might give, or a newspaper editorial, or even an essay that might appear in a school textbook to persuade kids of something. Be creative, and be utterly convincing. Remember—the purpose of propaganda is to spread information, ideas or rumors, in order to help one institution, or cause, or person—or to harm a different one."

He pauses, and then adds, "Sometimes the information in propaganda is true, but sometimes it's based on false rumors. In other words, you can lie. But—if you lie, and someone finds out it's a lie, you've undercut your cause severely. So—pick a cause. It can be anything from more pizza in the cafeteria to revitalizing the space program. We'll exchange propaganda tomorrow, and see whether or not you've convinced anybody—especially me. For tonight—start reading *The Ugly American*."

I stare at the blackboard, thinking about propaganda. I wonder if it's only people like the Nazis who use it, or if people use propaganda in little, everyday things as well. *Of course people use it every day. You know that,* Luke reminds me. *You hear it all the time.* But I don't want to follow his train of thought, so I concentrate on the essay.

Could I ever persuade anybody else to agree with something I believe? Teddy would love this assignment, but I'm not even sure what I believe—except that pictures matter. They matter because they tell the truth, because they don't lie.

I gnaw on the pencil for a while, then begin making notes about how photography tells the truth, trying to ig-nore the wish that I could discuss the idea with Teddy—and trying to ignore Mr. Mitchell's eyes on me, willing me to talk to him, or to a counselor. Maybe that's what he'd write for his propaganda if he were doing the assignment himself. Would it be truths or convincing lies he'd use to push his cause?

under suspicion

After class I try to eat some lunch, but the chicken nuggets taste greasy and the salad is warm and limp. I manage a few bites before my stomach churns, then clear out of the cafeteria. I go to pick up books for the afternoon, planning to hide out in the publications room for the rest of the lunch period. I'll work out a way to get into the hideout for the journals before the sheriff's deputies look hard enough to find them. Today they're busy dragging the river.

"There you are, Ian. I've been looking for you." Yesterday Sheriff Reynolds' deep voice was almost gentle. Now it sounds skeptical, as if he suspected he might not find me in school at all. I stop and turn to look at him.

"I was in Mr. Mitchell's class," I say, trying to sound confident because it's the truth. "Then lunch."

"And now you're at your locker," he finishes for me. "Books for afternoon classes?" He studies me, and I feel so tired, trying to stand there looking like the normal school Ian for him. Not enough sleep last night, and my backpack weighs a ton. I can't think what I should say to make him go away.

"What do you want?" I ask unsteadily.

He studies me through clinical eyes. "I want to find out what happened to Teddy Camden," he says softly. "Investigative work is largely a matter of hunches, Ian. You get a hunch, you check it out, you find what you're looking for. I've got a hunch you were hiding something when we talked yesterday. I want to find out what it is."

"I told you about the hideout," I point out.

"Yes, you did," he agrees. "But I have a hunch that's not all you were hiding." He waits for me to say (confess?) something, and when I don't, he sighs. "You did finally show me the contents of your backpack yesterday, so maybe what you're hiding is in your locker. Your father authorized me to look anywhere in the school I need to, which includes lockers, but perhaps you'd like to make things easier by opening it for me?"

I nearly refuse, but what's the point? He'd just force the lock, or get Dad to open it, which would be worse. I slowly spin the combination. And there's Teddy's camera, in plain sight.

"I thought you always carried your camera with you," the sheriff says thoughtfully. He peers at it more closely, then turns to look back to me. "It looks as if my hunch paid off—this isn't yours at all, is it? Whose camera is this, Ian?"

"It's Teddy's," I admit, my voice strange, almost hollow, in my ears. I reach in to hand it to him, but he puts one hand out to stop me. He takes a clear plastic bag out of one pocket and nudges the camera inside it. He stands there for a moment, looking from it to me. Then he beckons. "Come with me."

I follow him to an empty classroom, which he unlocks with a master key he must have gotten from Dad. "Tell me about this camera," he says, shutting the door behind us. "Did Teddy give it to you?"

I shake my head helplessly. "I don't know. I don't think so. I found it in my backpack yesterday morning."

"What do you mean—you don't know?" The sheriff's eyes burn into me. "The camera was in your backpack, and you don't know how it got there? You expect me to believe that?"

"It's the truth," I insist. "The camera was in my pack when I opened it, and I don't know how it got there."

Sheriff Reynolds turns the bagged camera over in his hands, his eyes narrowed. "All right—suppose I buy that." But he clearly doesn't. "Why didn't you tell me about it yesterday?"

Because I can't see any way around it, I tell him the truth. "I didn't know what was in the camera. I had to look at it first."

"And you did?"

I nod.

"What did you see?"

I shake my head. "Nothing."

He raises his chin skeptically. Teddy does the same thing sometimes. "If you erased the photos," he says, almost conversationally, "the forensic lab will find the altered memory, and I can charge you with destruction of evidence."

I feel my eyes widen. I knew better than to trust him this time, but I feel almost as if I've been blindsided again. "But I didn't!"

The sheriff sighs. "I know you're smart, Ian." How can he possibly think he knows that? I'm not smart enough to figure out what Cal meant—I'm not smart enough to understand my own dreams—I'm not as smart as Dad, or Teddy, or this man standing in front of me. "But our computer experts are smart too. They can recover erased memory."

"I hope they can." I mean it, fervently. "I sure can't. And I want to know what's in Teddy's camera" (what happened when I was zoned out) "just as much as they do—more."

"Yesterday, I might have agreed with you."

That must have been before I confirmed his "hunch" about hiding things. He shifts gears and asks, "You saw the newspaper this morning?"

I nod, reluctantly.

"You saw that photograph of Fern Grove?"

I nod, again.

"Have you seen that place before?"

How can I tell him I saw Teddy there in a dream? He'll think I'm crazy, and maybe I am. How can I say Teddy begged me to come find him? "It looked familiar," I hedge. "Teddy and I must have gone there sometime, shooting pictures."

"When?" Sheriff Reynolds asks quickly.

I give a half shrug, not knowing what to answer. Suddenly I feel how big he is, even bigger than Dad, and I'm all alone in this room with him. "I don't know when."

Then I remember he's taken the things in the hideout. "You'll see the pictures we took in the albums," I say in a rush.

He cocks his head to one side. "That's what I would have thought," he says in that slow, deep voice. "But there weren't any photos of Fern Grove in the albums. Why is that, I wonder?"

"I don't know," I hear myself say, as if from a distance. "It looked familiar."

"I have a hunch that's because you've been there recently."

"No," I tell him.

"Like—Monday afternoon?" he tells me, his voice hardening.

"No," I repeat, but my voice is shaky.

"You went there with Teddy, didn't you?" He towers over me, his thick eyebrows drawn together angrily.

"I didn't!" I try to insist, but I'm not completely sure—Teddy calling to me in the dream—the newspaper.

And then the sheriff pulls the floor out from under me and I'm falling, like Teddy in the dream. "The two of you went to Fern Grove on Monday to see that old derelict, Sawyer, didn't you?"

I'm too stunned to even shake my head. "Who? S-Sawyer?"

"Clement Sawyer," the sheriff says impatiently. "He's been hiding out in an old logging cabin in the forest." He pauses. "And when a boy disappears in the forest without a trace, it casts a suspicious light on Sawyer's presence, wouldn't you say?"

I swallow, unsure how to reply. "I don't know anybody named Clement Sawyer."

His eyes narrow, and he shakes Teddy's camera at me. "Don't lie to me, Ian. Tampering with evidence, lying to an investigating officer—you're a minor, but this might be a good moment to remind you that juvenile detention facilities exist for the express purpose of dealing with minors who break the law."

I know he's threatening me, but I don't see what I can do about it. Any of it. "I've never heard that name before," I insist. "But I know the guy—at least, I think I do. That's not what he told us to call him, though."

The sheriff digests this. "What name did he give you?"

"Cal Samuels."

"He's a cagey one," the sheriff comments. "When we went to the cabin to question him yesterday, he'd already cleared out, as if he knew to expect us." Then he fixes his stare on me again. "So you admit you know him?"

I nod, helplessly. "Yes, Teddy and I both know him."

"And you went to see him? Did Teddy think Sawyer was his father? Is that why you two went to see him?" Before I can answer, he presses, "Could he have put Teddy's camera in your pack?"

I think of the way Cal just appears and disappears. Could he have put it there while I was zoned out? "Maybe," I admit slowly.

"Or someone else," the sheriff suggests.

I remember Luke saying he'd done it, but I don't see how he could have. Talking to me is one thing, but some-how taking action—

The sheriff breaks into my confused silence. "You found it at school—could one of the students have put it there?"

Of course! Relief washes over me. Not Luke, not me— one of the students! Maybe Craig did it, for a laugh. But how could he have gotten it in the first place? I can't work through the questions. I finally say, "I don't know."

He sighs. "All right—back to Cal. I had a hunch you'd seen him this week. When?"

"I went to see him yesterday, after school." Well, it was

after school before I found him, so it's not exactly a lie.

The sheriff's expression sharpens. "Yesterday? In addition to Monday? Why did you go see him yesterday?"

"I just thought he might know something about Teddy," I explain awkwardly, not bothering to repeat that I hadn't seen him Monday. "I thought—well, maybe Teddy might have gone to him for help, if he couldn't find me."

"And why didn't you bother mentioning him when you told me everything you knew yesterday morning?"

"I wanted to see if he'd tell me what happened to Teddy," I say, hearing how dumb it sounds. The school Ian is supposed to be smart, but the sheriff is turning me into the stupid failure Ian.

"Something he wouldn't tell me or my deputies?" When I don't answer, he goes on, his voice sarcastic. "And what revealing truths did he tell you?"

There's no way I can explain Cal's word games when even I don't understand what he meant. "Nothing, really," I mumble. "He—well, he doesn't make much sense even when he does say something. Teddy could understand him, but I couldn't."

"He did talk to you, though," the sheriff says quickly, pouncing on me like a cat on a trapped mouse. "What did he say? Even if it didn't make any sense?"

"Just—he told me to read about Sherlock Holmes at Reichenbach Falls."

"That didn't mean anything to you at all?" he presses.

I shrug one shoulder. "I looked it up at home—everybody thought Sherlock Holmes was dead after he went off the cliff at Reichenback Falls. But he wasn't." I hesitate, then finish, "I thought maybe he meant Teddy was okay, and would be coming back, like Holmes."

"Did you?" he asks, skeptical. He studies me for a while, as if he's trying to decide whether or not I'm lying. "You want to know what I think, Ian?" He leans closer to me, his voice low and cold. I don't want to know, but he tells me anyway. "I have a hunch you went to find Sawyer yesterday to tell him not to say anything to us."

That's crazy, I want to tell him. Cal doesn't need me or anyone else to tell him what to say to whom! But the sheriff just goes on, "Was that why he hit the road before we could question him?"

"I just wanted him to tell me if he knew anything about Teddy!" My voice comes out high, almost hysterical.

"And why wouldn't you trust us to get that information out of him better than you could?" the sheriff demands. "I've got a hunch you were afraid he could tell us something you didn't want us to know—something you're still trying to hide." I'm beginning to hate his hunches. "Maybe you're the one who fought with Teddy on Monday and Sawyer witnessed it," he goes on, accusing, condemning, just like Dad.

"No!"

But Mr. Mitchell suggested the same thing. Did we fight? Is that what I did when I zoned out? I can't believe it—I don't want to believe it. But I can't explain any of this to Sheriff Reynolds, because he's already judged and convicted me. Before he can pile on more accusations, the classroom door bangs open and Dad stands there. Behind him I see curious faces, Sara's among them.

"What do you think you're doing, Sheriff Reynolds?" Dad demands. "You have no authority to question students without their parents' presence or permission." I feel limp with relief that Dad's behind me, protecting me.

"I was just continuing our conversation from yesterday," the sheriff says. "You didn't seem to have any problems with me talking to your son then."

"That was in my office," Dad tells him crisply, "not hidden away in a deserted classroom."

"I had a hunch that Ian was hiding something that I needed for my investigation," the sheriff says. He holds up Teddy's camera. "I found this in his locker. He claims it just appeared in his backpack yesterday morning."

I look at Dad, praying he'll stay on my side, not daring to offer any explanation.

Dad frowns at me, then up at the sheriff. "What made you think Ian was hiding anything? You questioned him yesterday—and you saw his camera then."

Sheriff Reynolds nods. "I did. But this is Teddy Camden's camera." He lets that sink in for a moment, and Dad's expression clearly lets me know I've let him down again. "Mrs. Camden said he never went anywhere without it. When she described it, however, I knew it wasn't the one I'd seen yesterday. I expected to find it at the Fern Grove site, but there was no sign of it when we dragged the river."

Dad looks taken aback. The sheriff continues, "Mrs. Camden also mentioned that Teddy and Ian often traded cameras, so I theorized that Ian might be—well, keeping it safe for his friend."

Dad turns his frown from Sheriff Reynolds to me. "The sheriff asked yesterday whether Teddy had been in contact with you," he says, his voice clear and deliberate. I'm sure all the kids in the hallway can hear every word. "You lied to him."

Dad puts one heavy hand on my shoulder, a jailer now, instead of a protector. "I apologize for my son, Sheriff," he says, his tone resigned. "You try as hard as you can to bring a boy up right, and then he falls in with bad company and turns into a liar. Do you have to charge him with anything?"

I feel greasy chicken nuggets churning in my stomach. How could holding onto Teddy's camera be so serious?

Sheriff Reynolds studies me. He and Dad both look used to intimidating people with their bulk, and I feel trapped between them. Then the sheriff sighs, his bushy eyebrows tightening into a frown. "Ian, I could charge you with withholding evidence, you know."

"But—"

Dad's hand tightens on my shoulder, and I shut up, feeling the tension vibrating through his arm into me.

"But I have the camera now, Mr. Slater, and I don't think I need to take Ian in just yet." He inclines his head to Dad, whose grip relaxes slightly. The two of them smile, two strong men who each understand the other perfectly.

"But I'll be keeping an eye on you, Ian," Sheriff Reynolds tells me, his voice a threat again. Then he goes out of the classroom, and the pack of students in the hallway parts for him.

The second Sheriff Reynolds closes the door behind him, Dad turns on me. "What were you doing with Teddy's camera?" he demands, his voice barely above a harsh whisper. I can see some faces through the window in the door, but all they'll be able to make out is his back. They might even think he's leaning over me to make sure I'm all right.

"I'm sorry," I stammer, feeling cold inside. Dad's never lit into me at school before. He's always been too conscious of presenting his public self as the concerned, caring principal—every student's pal.

"You're sorry," he mimics, furious. I can't see how to answer him, knowing the kids are watching, wondering what they can hear. I try to keep my voice as low as his. "I—I had my own camera with me. I don't know how Teddy's got into my backpack—it was just there when I opened it yesterday morning."

"And you didn't bother to mention it to Reynolds when he questioned you? Don't you realize how guilty that makes you look?"

"But—I didn't do anything! He didn't ask about Teddy's camera!" I try to explain.

"He didn't ask! That's no excuse—you told him all about your little hideout and your precious redwoods photography." He glares at me, then sighs, his shoulders sagging a little. "I wish I could teach you how to grow up, Ian. You think now that you want to be a photographer, but that's no lifetime career. When I was your age, I wanted to be a park ranger—did you know that?"

I look up at him in surprise. I don't think he ever told me that before. Was that because his father used to map the forest before he died?

Dad goes on, "But how was I supposed to make something of myself and support a family as a park ranger? It was a crazy, selfish dream and I gave it up. Being a teacher, a principal, becoming superintendent—that's a career, a way a man can make a difference in the world, raising other people's kids right, taking care of his family at the same time. You need to stop playing games in the forest like a child and make something of yourself—and lying to the sheriff only makes you a criminal. So why did you do it?"

He waits for an answer. "I thought—maybe—Teddy left me a message in the camera." It sounds so lame.

"And did he?"

I shake my head. "No."

"Of course he didn't." Dad sounds more tired than angry now. "Why should he? Do you think he actually liked you?"

I can't speak, and the pause drags out. Where is Luke to contradict him? But Luke always disappeared before when Dad showed up. Why should now be any different? Dad expects an answer. I reach into someplace deep inside to drag words to the surface. "I don't know," I finally manage.

"How stupid are you, Ian? You're the better photographer—you're the one whose pictures make the *Sawville Journal*." Dad shakes his head, pityingly. "He takes half the credit for your work on the yearbook and the school paper, and you don't even realize he's using you."

He can't be right, can he? But if we really were friends like I thought, why did Teddy go off without me? I never could understand why he liked me. He's clever and could have plenty of other friends. I stare at the scuffed floor tiles, feeling the backpack's dead weight pulling me down.

"Teddy doesn't have a father to give a damn about him," Dad says, and his voice turns bitter. "You're a sorry piece of work, but you should be grateful that you have a father whose job it is to protect you."

He stares at me for a minute, then walks out of the

room, closing the door firmly behind him.

I stand there, looking out the windows to the redwoods across the parking lot. The trees blur, and I feel as if I'm staring at a picture too close up, where all you can see is millions of pixels, each one so tiny and bright that your eye can't combine them to see the pattern they form. One group of pixels might tell me what happened to Teddy, if only I could see them clearly. A different cluster would let me see what Cal knows, and another scattering would show me how the camera got into my backpack.

Is the sheriff right? Did I put the camera in my pack myself? Did I put it there while I was in the zone, after I pushed Teddy down into the river's rushing current?

I don't know what I'm supposed to do. Does Dad mean me to stay in the empty classroom and think about what I've done, like shutting the failure Ian in the closet at home? I blink, and the redwood giants swim back into focus, as permanent as Dad's dream of becoming the perfect superintendent with the perfect family. I wish I could see as clearly how to prove myself the son he needs, and at the same time give Teddy the help he needs.

a different hideout

I finally pick up a late pass from Mrs. Feeney, then go through the motions in Mrs. Harley's class, hiding out in the back of the room and not really concentrating on math. I have gym last period, but I get a pass out. I bypass study hall—I just can't face the other kids, not even Sara—and bike out to the motel.

I cruise by casually the first time, in case the sheriff's deputies are still there. Teddy would be proud of how careful I am (except for telling them where the hideout was in the first place, of course). But everyone's gone—no sign of policemen or deputies in the center cabin that was the front office, no sign of cars in the parking lot.

Redwood Reststop is one of those old roadside motels with a half circle of little individual tan stucco bungalows with green or brown trim—an illusion of privacy among the redwoods. Actually, the cabins curve back on each other, with the parking lot stretching around the front, and they're all connected along the back wall for the plumbing, though that's long since been shut off. You can't see it from the outside, but Teddy knew how the crawl spaces linked up.

Amazingly, none of the windows have been broken and boarded up—I guess there wouldn't be any glass left in them if this place was closer to a big city. But here the windows just look streaked and dusty in the afternoon sunlight. Most of them still have dirty mesh curtains hanging from sagging rods.

A twisted band of yellow-and-black police tape surrounds the green-trimmed entrance and windows of cabin 17. I make sure no one's looking, then duck under the tape. I try the door handle, but the deputies left it locked. I still have the copy of the master key Teddy made for me, though, so that's not a problem. I quickly unlock the cabin and slip inside with the bike, locking the door behind me.

It's normally dusty and shadowy inside, lit only by the light from the windows until we turn on the battery-powered light. Most of the furniture is missing. When we first checked out the place, cabin 17 had a few broken chairs, a rickety, sagging table, and a broken bed frame. We scoured the rest of the cabins for some chairs that would hold us, careful to go in and out when no one was driving by. It took a while, but we finally found enough stuff. We even found two tables that were pretty solid, once we braced one unsteady leg. And there's a built-in counter along the back wall beside the bathroom—we use that to stack photo books and magazines. It hurts to remember the two of us working together, like friends, after Dad said we couldn't ever have been friends at all.

But it's still the most comfortable hideout I've ever had—the wallpaper's only peeling a little (we stuck the loose parts back on with superglue), and we printed out all our best photos and hung them up everywhere. We've got all the comforts of home—under the counter we stashed a supply of paper plates and paper towels and sodas and munchies. We bought a metal box for the chips and cookies and stuff, so the food wouldn't attract animals, and even cleaned the place so it wouldn't smell musty.

Now the room looks like a tornado hit it. The furniture has been shoved around, and all the books and magazines are gone. The deputies even took the photos we had on the walls, and the albums we'd left out. I prop the bike up by the door and leave my pack beside it. I don't light the lamp. I can find my way to the back of the room by the faint sunlight coming through the mesh curtains. In the shadows I see the bar for hanging clothes that's on the wall opposite the bathroom door. Teddy and I hang jeans and T-shirts and sweatshirts there so we can change from school clothes before going into the forest, but the deputies have taken them all.

They left the munchies and drinks. I see a bottle of raspberry flavored water, Teddy's favorite, and my stomach suddenly convulses and burns. I hug myself tightly, trying to stop the relentless barrage of images—Teddy, tipping up a bottle of water and drinking thirstily after a hike through the redwoods—Teddy, peering at my iBook screen, tapping keys as he programs our cameras—Teddy, looking through his camera up into the trees—Teddy, studying me through his viewfinder—Teddy, bent over his journal—

Teddy, my friend. I came for the journals, especially *his* journals. If the sheriff's deputies search the other cabins thoroughly, they might find them.

I go into the bathroom. I guess they took a quick look in here, then dismissed it since the plumbing doesn't work anymore. I study the maintenance panel carefully, but I don't think they messed with it. I go back to the bike and strip off the school clothes I'm wearing so they won't get filthy in the crawl space. I drape them over the seat and get the small flashlight I carry in my backpack. It's on a key ring with a little tool that doubles as a screwdriver and a can opener. I use the screwdriver to take the screws out of the maintenance panel, then swing it open and climb in, lighting the dusty tunnel with the flashlight. It leads into cabin 16, where the panel just leans up against the opening, hidden behind a lot of old furniture. We set it up this way—well, I did mostly. Teddy teased me that I worried too much about hiding our stuff. But I hid it as if I wanted to hide it from Dad. Teddy would be glad now, since the deputies took everything in the other cabin.

When I come out into cabin 16, I can see stuff's been moved around a little. I leave food in here every now and then, so that animals like raccoons and squirrels can get in and mess up the dust. That way our footprints don't stand out. The deputies must have come in the front door of the cabin and not have noticed anything strange, because they didn't climb through all the cabin's junk clear to the back.

I tilt a broken bed frame in the opposite direction to rest against a couple of three-legged chairs instead of the sagging table. Then I slip between the table and the frame, ease myself behind an old chest of drawers, and step over a warped floor lamp. I move a broken chair from where it rests against a sagging cabinet and open the cabinet door. It's so dark, the inside looks empty. But when I lift out the black cloth I'd found in the remnants box at the discount store, it exposes a couple of albums and our journals.

Mrs. Stillman, our seventh-grade English teacher, started us on the journals. We'd done a little journal writing in elementary school, but Mrs. Stillman's journaling was different. She had us read selections from real writers' journals, and she let us write whatever we wanted, whenever we wanted, just like them. She didn't read the entries, either, just the parts we turned in to be graded. Teddy got hooked on writing for the fun of it—putting into words the things he didn't like to talk about any more than I did. Like photography, it was something we had in common, one more reason I want to believe Dad has to be wrong—Teddy and I really are friends.

We kept writing journals even after we didn't have to, but we hid them here. I pull out the stack of notebooks and albums and make my way back to the bathroom, not bothering to camouflage the hiding place this time. I don't care if the deputies realize someone's been in here. What matters is keeping Teddy's journal safe—and finding out if it says what he was going to do or who he was going to meet. I push the pile of notebooks and albums unsteadily through the crawl space, gather them up on the far side, and take them over to the bike.

Then I realize I haven't brought anything to tie them onto the bike carrier rack. Stupid! Every time I think I've got a plan I run up against the reality that I just can't do anything right, like Dad says. But I have to do something with the journals and albums, now that I've taken them out of their hiding place. Finally I dig into my backpack and pull out the long phone cable I carry for going online. I twist it around and around the journals and albums on the carrier rack. Then I try to wipe enough dust off myself to put the school clothes back on without getting them filthy after all.

I look through the mesh curtains, studying the road carefully, but I can't see anyone out there. Finally I open the door and push the bike out quickly. Then I lock up and slip back under the yellow-and-black tape. No one jumps out to arrest me, and I make it to the street and start pedaling south, farther away from town.

Before I met Teddy, back when I was in elementary school, I had another hideout—an abandoned campsite, where lightning had struck this giant redwood. It crushed the wooden table and bench and blocked the rutted dirt driveway into the campsite, its branches pushed up against the cupboard that was supposed to keep campers' food from attracting wildlife. I found I could slip around back, hide the bike behind the fallen tree, and sit on the remnants of the bench. I could even use the part of the table still standing to write in the journal I was already keeping then—a way to wrap my memories in plastic and leave them behind in the cupboard.

I took Teddy there after we started working on the newspaper together, once I thought we were friends. He was amazed.

"You mean you come here every afternoon?" he asked, his eyes wide as he studied the place.

"Pretty much," I told him. "Except when it rains."

He nodded. "This is excellent—you can't even tell the campsite's here from the street." And he grinned that daring grin at me. "But I know somewhere we can go even if it rains."

I so envied the grin, and the courage behind it. Teddy

could dare anything—stuff I couldn't even imagine. I wanted to figure out how I could be like that. So I biked after him to the motel. Once we got it fixed up, we moved the stuff out of the old hideout into cabin 17.

But the ruined campsite and its wooden cupboard are still there, still hidden from the road, waiting for me the way the closet waits. I carefully unknot the telephone cord, coil it up, then stack the notebooks and albums in the cupboard. That will keep them safe for now, but it's not waterproof if it rains. I'll have to get some plastic to wrap them.

I save out Teddy's journal and the top album. We hang some of the redwood photos in our hideout, but these albums are for other pictures, like close-ups of a fern through bike spokes, or experiments with light and texture, or spectacular mistakes (like my early shot of Teddy with a Douglas fir growing out of his head). I flip to the last photo I took of Teddy, just two weeks ago. I realize with a pang that he looks almost like a stranger already. He's standing on top of a fallen redwood log in the old forest, his arms upraised, fingers stretched toward the sky, as if he could touch the tips of the redwoods. Late-afternoon golden light silhouettes him, turning his frizzy hair the color of the red heartwood of the trees that surround him. It's hard to shoot a silhouette, because the sun shining at your subject is shining in your lens. The trick is to stand in the shadows.

Facing that photo is a shot Teddy took of me. I'm leaning against the base of a giant redwood in Fern Grove.

Of course we've been there. We've explored it and photographed it—only the photos are in here, in these albums, not the ones the police took. In the picture, I've got my hands clasped around my knees, and I'm looking down, sort of. Teddy has the color balance just right—you can see the face standing out, pale against brown-streaked tree bark ridges and dark blue sweatshirt sleeves. You can only see the eyes on an angle, but the picture makes me want to cry. The eyes are squeezed shut—not just against the sunlight, against something the boy in the picture doesn't want to see.

Did Teddy know, then, what things were like with me? Why didn't he say anything? Was he trying to show how small and insignificant I was? He did a good job, but it hurts that he showed me so clearly. Or maybe Teddy didn't realize how honest the picture was—maybe it was the camera that saw me. Dad must have been right—he was just using me to get ahead in his own photography. I can't quite imagine Teddy doing that, but I can't see how Dad could be wrong about it.

I put the album inside the cupboard and reach for Teddy's journal. Then I see the slanting sun. How late is it? Grandmother's coming to supper, and I've got to get home in time to clean up before she arrives. There's no time to see what Teddy wrote—I shouldn't have wasted time looking at the album! I could take the journal home to read after supper. But what if Dad chooses tonight to check through my backpack? Maybe I can come back later tonight.

I slam the cupboard door closed, jam some stout fallen branches tightly against it, and pedal away from the campsite and its secrets. After breaking out of the rutted trails through the trees, I fly down the road, dodging onto the shoulder for the few cars that pass me. Unexpectedly, I see Dad's SUV up ahead. The brake lights come on, and he pulls over into a parking area. I slow down, dreading his anger at my wasting time in the forest when I should have been home early. His door opens, and he climbs out. He's changed from his school suit into jeans and a sweatshirt, and he cocks one eyebrow at the wrinkled school clothes I'm wearing, dusty in spite of my efforts. To my surprise, however, he says nothing about them.

"I thought you'd be out here. I took a chance I might run into you." He smiles and I smile back, grateful that he doesn't sound upset. At the same time, I can't help thinking that two people have to know each other pretty well— or be really lucky—to just run into each other out here, as big as the forest is.

Before I can apologize for not going straight home, Dad asks, "Want to walk a little?" I nod, surprised at the unexpected, easy forgiveness, but wanting to accept the shift away from his anger in school. It's been ages since we've gone for walks in the forest together. He's been too busy with work, and I've been hiding out with Teddy. Without our walks, all we've had was my letting him down and his deepening disappointment in me.

He puts the bike and my pack in the back of the SUV, and I'm relieved I left Teddy's journal safe in the cupboard. Then he locks up and picks a trail that's broad enough, near the road at least, for us to walk side by side.

Just as I'm about to apologize once more for Teddy's camera, Dad surprises me again. "I was hoping I'd find you, because I wanted to tell you I was sorry about losing my temper with you in school." He sounds as if he's having trouble forcing the words out. Dad hates apologizing, for anything.

"No," I say quickly, "it was my fault, for not saying anything yesterday about the camera. I'm sorry."

Dad shoots me a sideways look. "Yes, it was your fault. But—well, I overreacted." He sighs heavily. "I've been under a lot of stress recently, Ian, and this thing with your friend disappearing—it's put a lot of pressure on me that I just didn't need. I know it's not all your fault," he adds quickly, "and I shouldn't let myself fly off the handle so easily, but—" He breaks off and stops walking. He rests one hand against the shaggy bark of a towering redwood. When he speaks again, his voice is soft enough that I have to lean closer to make out the words. "You can't imagine how much the superintendent position means to me."

I want to tell him that I can imagine it—as much as becoming a really good photographer means to me, as much as getting away from the home where I always feel such a failure means. Only, right at this moment, I don't want to get away from Dad, or home. As long as I don't say anything about my photography—or Teddy—there doesn't seem to be any chasm distancing us from each other.

Dad sighs and straightens up, pointing. "You know what's down there?"

I look, but the old-growth forest is so thick here I can't see very far. "No—what?"

He smiles. "Listen." And then I hear it, faintly, underneath the soft rustling of the branches and the tan oak leaves on the breeze—the restless gurgling of the river.

"That's where the river curves back around, isn't it?" I ask.

He smiles, pleased that I recognized it. "That's right."

"How did you know that?"

Dad starts walking again. "When I used to go for walks with my father, he'd follow any rut that even looked like it might have once been a trail. I think he showed me every shortcut and backway that's ever been tramped through the forest."

And he's never forgotten. Is it the trails he remembers, or the time with his father? I think of Teddy, wanting so badly to find his father, and then think how I'd feel without Dad—freed from the fear of letting him down, yes, but also adrift, missing him, wanting him. "You miss him, don't you?" I ask, not thinking first. Then I realize with a chill that it might have been the wrong thing to say.

Unexpectedly, Dad laughs. "Miss him? I don't miss him at all." He looks at me, his eyes turning hard. "He walked out on us, my mother and me, Ian. Just announced he was leaving." His eyes slide away, looking through the redwoods, far into the mist. "I was nine. No explanation, no apologies, just good-bye. It was January, and my mother was discussing my grades with me." A faint, ironic smile crosses his face briefly, and I suspect he remembers her telling him that his grades weren't good enough. "My father just stood there in the doorway, listening. I thought he might tell her to ease up—say something like, hey, it's only fourth grade, after all, but he never interrupted. He just waited until there was a pause. And then he said, 'I'm leaving now. Good-bye.' And he turned and went out."

I ask, hoping not to break the spell, but desperate to know. "And you didn't ever see him again?"

Dad comes back from the redwood mist and looks at me. "Mother refused to let him bother me. And I didn't want anything to do with him. He sent things—cards and parcels. Mother left them out for me, but I just marked them 'Return to Sender' and dropped them in the mailbox. But I did see him again. He came to my high school graduation. He went on about how proud he was of me and how sorry he was he hadn't been able to be there to watch me grow up." Dad snorts, shaking his head. "He made his choice, and I made mine."

But I wondered if it was really that simple. Maybe Dad had never forgiven his father for leaving—or for not taking him when he got out. And maybe Dad regretted his anger, but didn't know how to change things.

Impulsively, as I try to match his strides through the duff, I say, "Too bad this isn't a cornfield instead of a redwood forest."

When he shoots me a quizzical glance over his shoulder I quote from *Field of Dreams*, one of the sports movies we'd watched together. "You know: 'If you build it, he will come.' Maybe he did miss you and just didn't know how to make up for leaving."

Dad doesn't say anything for a minute, and I'm afraid I've gone too far. I expect him to be furious, but all he says is, "Don't be ridiculous, Ian." Then he laughs, shaking his head. "You're such an idealist! I don't know where you get it from." My knees feel weak with relief that he's amused instead of angry.

Dad keeps walking, still chuckling. "I'm afraid the cornfield trick only works for ghosts, and my father isn't dead."

Grandfather is still alive?

I catch myself before my feet come to a complete stop right in the middle of the path, and manage to keep up with Dad. I don't know what to make of the discovery that

I'm part of a larger family than I realized.

Dad goes on, not noticing my shock. "He wanted to come to my wedding, can you believe it? I told him absolutely not, of course. He was the last person I wanted to see there. What did he know about marriage and family? Your mother's never met him. And you won't, either. I forbid it." I nod automatically, but I can't understand how you can just cut someone off completely, no matter what they've done.

Then I recall his saying, long ago, that he wished I'd known Grandfather. Maybe Dad thinks he doesn't ever want to see his own father again—and wants to make peace with him at the same time. Maybe we can want contradictory things, the way I want to escape, and to go on walking here in the woods with Dad forever.

trapped

I see Grandmother's car parked in front of the house as we pull into the driveway, and remember that I'd wanted to clean up before she saw me. Too late now. I glance at Dad, reaching for the closeness we shared in the forest, but he's distant again as he unbuckles his seatbelt, climbs out, and pulls the bike out of the back. I park it by the side of the garage, lock it, and follow him inside.

"Chris? Ian? Is that you?" Her voice screeches like chalk on a blackboard.

Dad turns reluctantly and we go into the living room. "Hello, Mother," he says, bending to kiss her cheek. There's no sign of Mom. She's probably in the kitchen, working on supper.

"Hi, Grandmother," I say, watching her closely as Dad straightens up. Most days I keep my eye on him to see how I'm supposed to feel and how I should react, as if he's a weather report telling me whether I should take pictures outside or indoors. But when Grandmother comes to supper, she's the one I check for the evening forecast.

"Good heavens, child, you look a wreck!" She turns to my father, who's crossed to his recliner, although he's sitting ramrod straight in it instead of reclining. "Chris, how can you just let the boy run wild and get filthy like that?" She turns back to me, her gray eyes bright under frosted hair. She looks like a fairly typical grandmother, I guess—frail and bony, so that her clothes hang on her more every year, but inside she's stronger than anyone else in the family. Her mind is still sharp, too, and she slices away at each of us with it.

"Go up and change, Ian," Dad says, his voice expressionless.

Tonight I'm supposed to be the good grandson, unappreciated by his parents. Dad will take it out on me later, but Grandmother is in charge for now. And it's better than the nights when I'm the worthless grandson, ruined by a worthless father.

It's tempting to change as slowly as possible, but not worth it. She'll just complain if I don't hurry, so I throw the dirty clothes in the hamper, pull on what I'll wear to school tomorrow, and head back downstairs.

"There—that's better," Grandmother says, smiling. She points to one of the good chairs, and I perch carefully on its edge. The living room is a formal room full of dark mahogany furniture covered in uncomfortable upholstery, with a fringed Oriental rug over the hardwood floor and an elaborately carved fireplace above a marble hearth. The curtains are always drawn, and the room looks dark even during the day, unless Dad turns on the table lamps.

I'm more used to looking at the room from the outside—nights when it's just us at home, Dad says it's a room for civilized people, and I don't qualify. But Grandmother always wants to sit in here and expects me to join her. She almost acts as if she thinks Dad's the one who doesn't deserve to sit here with us.

"I just can't get over it," she goes on, "your father playing out in the forest with you like an overgrown irresponsible child!" She looks at Dad sitting stiffly in his recliner. "Honestly, Chris," she tells him, "a son—such a precious gift! You can't just let him run wild."

"I don't let him run wild," Dad says, between clenched teeth.

"Well then, you run wild with him," Grandmother retorts. "After all the effort I put into watching over you, I'd have thought you'd be a stronger father."

He *is* strong, I want to say. But my opinion would just make things worse. Is this why Grandfather left? Because he couldn't stand listening to her like this, night after night? Maybe he really did want to take Dad with him, but it took all the strength he had just to get himself out the door.

"Of course, you were always running off yourself," she continues. "Off every afternoon with undesirable friends, instead of home helping your mother. So—what can I expect? Like father, like son."

I try to imagine Dad having friends and fail, even though I've heard over and over how Dad let her down by hanging out with kids she disapproved of. Did she lock him in the closet to think about how he could be a better son? Was that why he escaped into the redwoods? I wonder what Grandmother's mom or dad must have done to her, and sigh.

"Now look," she says, "you're upsetting the boy!" And she starts fussing over me. "Tell me, Ian, what have you been up to? I haven't seen your name in the paper recently—you're such a good photographer! I tell everyone my grandson is going to be taking pictures for the *National Geographic* one day soon! So—how's your photography doing?"

"Fine," I tell her. I should like it when she talks like that, but I don't believe she means it. Praising me is just another way to get at Dad. I tell her, as if I'm mouthing lines written by somebody else, "I've been working on the yearbook at school mostly."

"Good for you!" Grandmother beams at me. "That yearbook would just fall apart without real talent like yours." She frowns at Dad. "Is that strange man still running the newspaper and yearbook, Chris?"

"Yes," Dad says, his voice as disapproving as hers.

"You should fire him," she says firmly. "In my days I wouldn't have let someone like him be around impressionable young people." Grandmother retired as an assistant principal, but I can easily imagine her firing someone she didn't like, whether she had the authority or not.

Dad says, "In your days, firing didn't involve the legal issues it does now."

I wonder what legal issues could have to do with Mr. Mitchell—something about freedom of the press? I don't understand why the two of them dislike him so much.

"The yearbook is certainly a good stepping-stone," Grandmother is saying, "but it's not too soon to start thinking big, Ian. Otherwise you'll be stuck in this backwoods little town forever, like your father."

"Not forever," Dad says. "Once I start this superintendent job—"

"*If* it ever happens," she interrupts, shaking her head. "I wouldn't count on it, Chris. You know how you get your hopes up, then things fall through and you're all disappointed."

"This won't fall through," Dad says, almost to himself.

"If only you'd started teaching earlier," she tells him. She says it most nights she's over here. If he'd started sooner he'd be making more money, or he'd have a bigger house, or he'd have been promoted faster. Is that why Dad is so determined to become superintendent? Maybe he thinks Grandmother will be proud of him if he's more successful than she was in the same field. When he got to be principal, though, she just said that men were always promoted beyond women.

"But I can see that Ian's not going to stay in Sawville forever," she says, switching back to me. "He's already on the way to better things—look at that essay contest he won!" Grandmother looks at the mantle proudly. The plaque for last year's California state essay contest hangs above the fireplace. They also sent a silver grizzly bear trophy, which sits on the mantle. "You never won a prize in school, Chris."

I can see fury glinting in Dad's eyes, along with a shine of tears. I know how that feels, how words can burn and make you fight to keep from crying.

Every time Grandmother goes on about that award I think: yes, he did win a prize in school, Grandmother, you just don't know it. That's not my trophy or plaque there— they're his. I didn't write the winning essay, he did! But I can't shape the words to admit that I couldn't even write a stupid essay about California by myself.

But you could have, Luke whispers, surprising me by coming out so close to Dad. *You could have written about the redwoods, photo images in words.*

He's right. I remember starting to write the essay and feeling almost proud of my effort. But Dad said it wasn't good enough. He said it had to be the best—it would make him look good if I won. So he wrote it for me, and I copied it and turned it in, and the essay won. But it's his prize, Grandmother.

I can almost feel tears in my own eyes.

Dad demands, "What are you looking at? Do you want to take a damn picture?"

"Don't talk to the boy that way!" Grandmother snaps, and my stomach burns. I don't know how I'm going to make it through the pork roast. I wish I were back in the redwoods with Dad—only he doesn't stay the person he is when he's there with me. He changes when we come inside this house, the way the school Ian and the home Ian are two different people. I wish I were in the redwoods with someone who stayed the same person all the time—with Teddy, only Teddy's gone. Who does that leave? Luke?

How about Sara? Luke suggests. The idea surprises me, but he's right—she's always herself, friendly and bothersome and usually right. What would it be like to walk in the forest with her?

Before I lose myself imagining the image, the telephone rings. A moment later, Mom comes hesitantly to the living-room doorway.

"Chris? It's Mrs. Camden on the phone for you."

"Mrs.? Hah!" Grandmother says. Everyone in town knows that Teddy's mother hasn't ever been married.

People just call her "Mrs." to be polite.

Dad grunts and gets up to pick up the hall phone while Mom hurries back to the kitchen to hang up there. "Hello?" he says sharply. "What is it?"

I can't hear Mrs. Camden's side of the conversation, only Dad's—he sounds impatient and gruff. "Haven't you talked to Sheriff Reynolds? Well, he's the one you should call, not me. How would I know what he found out?"

Grandmother has half turned in her chair, watching him in the hallway. I frame a picture that shows her profile along the left side and upper corner, then Dad's back along the right side. Between them, beneath his hand holding the phone receiver, you can see the door to the storage closet.

"Of course I remember." Dad's voice is harsh. "But what does that matter now? What do you expect me to do about it? That's your problem, not mine."

Dad would never talk to any other parent that way. He always bends over backward to sound concerned and caring when a parent calls him. But he's never liked Teddy or his mother.

Grandmother snorts, shaking her head.

"Now don't get hysterical, Suzy," Dad says sharply. "Talk to Sheriff Reynolds. I'm sure he's doing everything he can."

I think again of the photo I took of Teddy and his mother. I remember her smothering him with hugs, but I also remember him telling me how she shrieked at him when she got drunk. I can easily imagine her being hysterical now that he's been gone since Monday.

Dad finally slams down the phone.

"Oh, with that caring attitude toward parents, the

school board is going to be overjoyed that they promoted you," Grandmother tells him.

Dad glares from her to me, then strides into the dining room. "Are we ever going to eat?" he demands.

Mom calls, "I'm just dishing things up, Chris," and Dad waves us into the room. My stomach cramps at the smell of the tart pork roast. Somehow, I survive the meal, accept the dry peck Grandmother calls a kiss, and escape upstairs.

I fire up my iBook and finish my propaganda homework. It's quiet with Dad still listening to Grandmother in the living room, and I sit there thinking about Teddy's journal. Maybe I can slip out after she leaves and Dad goes to bed. If I take a flashlight, I can read it at the campsite. My mind drifts into the plan, waiting for the sound of her car pulling out of the driveway. My fingers fiddle with the iBook absently—I almost feel as if I'm watching someone else hitting keys, and I can't even see the screen anymore. I just relax into the fog and zone out, not worrying about anything. I don't have to worry just now.

It's not a car spitting gravel, but heavy footfalls on the stairway that pull me out of the zone. I blink at the iBook. It shows the macro script Teddy wrote so I could upload my sports pictures directly to the newspaper. What's it doing on the screen? The footfalls get closer, climbing all the way to my room. I shut down the iBook, set my batteries to charge, and turn in time to see Dad standing in the doorway.

"What have you been doing?" he asks, his voice no relation to the friendly, laughing tone from the redwoods.

"Just my homework," I tell him, gesturing to the laptop. "I had an essay."

"Is it finished?"

"Yes, sir."

He nods sharply. "You embarrassed me with your grand-mother tonight. And you embarrassed me in front of the sheriff this afternoon."

I swallow. "I'm sorry." The words come out unsteadily.

He nods. "I'm sure you are. But being sorry doesn't seem to stop you from being an embarrassment, does it?" He's right about that.

Dad shakes his head. "I just don't know what to do with you, Ian. I try and I try, but you just keep letting me down." He looks around the room, coming full circle back to my iBook. "Maybe I've spoiled you, giving you everything you wanted. Maybe having fewer comforts would teach you better."

I stare at him, terrified that he'll take my iBook and camera. Who would I be without them? He steps into my room, and I almost beg him not to take them, not to make me smash them like the toy camera. But then he grips my arm instead, his fingers digging into the flesh. "Maybe the occasional hour in the closet isn't enough time for you to learn your lesson." He's pulling me downstairs as he speaks. "You'll sleep there tonight, Ian. Perhaps from now on."

Then we're standing at the open storage closet door, and I see he's placed a blanket inside. "If sleeping here doesn't help," he adds, "I'll remove the blanket. But let's see how you do."

I turn to him, weak with relief that he didn't take my laptop and camera, but also afraid. If I'm locked in all night—

He sees my eyes dart nervously to the bathroom. "I'm not surprised you can't hold it until morning." He pauses, watching my face redden, considering the problem. "Well, your mother doesn't need the extra work of cleaning up after you. And you don't really need me to lock this door to keep you where you belong the rest of the night, do you?"

"No, sir," I say quickly, and stoop down to go inside.

I'm sorry, Teddy—I can't get out to read your journal tonight. Even if you really are (were?) my friend, I can't help you now. I huddle in the corner of the closet, making myself as small as possible, hugging the blanket helplessly.

A dim image slips into my mind of a teddy bear I used to have—back before I started elementary school. I slept with Bear and carried him everywhere with me, even in the forest. Finally Dad took him away. "This thing is filthy! If you can't take care of it, you don't deserve to keep it."

I tried to hold onto Bear, but Dad said, "Do you want to be a baby all your life?" I shook my head, but I didn't let Bear go either. Dad said, "You act as if you love this toy better than you love your own family."

I wanted to say—Bear makes me feel safe in the dark. But Dad told me, "It's time for you to grow up, Ian. No one's going to believe I could be a good principal if my son won't throw away his baby toys." And he put me in the closet to think about it.

Luke was so upset he started shouting, almost before Dad was gone, *He can't do that! Bear is yours! Make him give Bear back!* But I made Luke shut up. I told myself not to cry in the closet, to feel safe there, and to turn off the part of me that cared about Bear. I didn't even let myself get distracted by imagining any cartoons or movies. I just sat in the dark and hugged my knees and kept telling myself in a low, hoarse, dragging whisper that I'd be fine without

Bear—I didn't need him—I did care more about Dad than a toy. Dad was the one I could trust to be there for me in the real world.

By the time Dad let me out and told me to throw Bear into the trash, I didn't feel the toy's soft, solid weight. I didn't feel anything. When I didn't cry, Dad even said, "I'm proud of you, Ian."

But later, after Teddy and I got to be friends, I saw his bedroom. He's got a faded plush dinosaur on one shelf that looks so squashed, he must sleep with it sometimes. A worn bear sits on another shelf. His mother didn't make him throw them away—and Teddy's not babyish. I'm not sure anymore that it really was such a terrible thing for me to want to keep Bear.

Then why had Dad insisted on taking him away from me?

I don't want to face the question. I don't want all these memories that keep intruding—they're the sort of memories I push out of mind in the shadowy corners of my head, or write in my journal so I can shut the cover on them. It's almost as if I'm not just the home Ian and the school Ian and the failure Ian these days—there's also this little-kid Ian inside of me who remembers everything I've tried to forget about growing up.

I try to sleep, but the memory of the newspaper story intrudes. I keep seeing Teddy struggling in my imagination—someone shaking him, pushing him, throwing him over the drop-off at Fern Grove. I see a rocky slope—a snapshot of scraped duff, exposed roots, and shadows; snapshots of Teddy falling, Teddy's body limp on the duff, Teddy dead—

I open damp eyes so I don't have to look. The sheriff's deputies have everything wrong if they think Teddy's dead, because Cal said that Sherlock Holmes at Reichenbach Falls would give me some ideas about Teddy, and he had to mean that Teddy wasn't dead—he had to!

I rock myself, hugging the blanket, until I slide into dreams of tangled shadow and light, hearing first Teddy's laughter and then his screams—dreams in which the towering redwoods in the grove turn into jail bars, imprisoning me until all I can do is reach helplessly between them, straining to catch Teddy, to keep him safe, while he calls again and again for me to come find him.

"Ian!"

I awaken, heart pounding, terrified it was Dad who shouted for me, but after a few moments I hear his snores upstairs. The cry came only from the Teddy of my dreams, and I'm safe in the dark closet.

What do you mean, safe? Luke demands, shocked. *Shut up in a closet instead of tucked in bed with Bear? How can you be safe? If you want to be safe, get out of there.*

What's wrong with you? I want to scream at him. *You're supposed to be my friend! You used to help me, not push me around like Dad and the sheriff and even Mr. Mitchell, all trying to make me do what they want. You used to—just let me be me.*

Everything's changed, Luke tries to explain. *You have to see that, Ian. I'm still here to help you, but now we've got to help Teddy, too. I know you want to, or else I wouldn't be here.*

Of course I do.

Then expose the truth.

That's what Teddy said in the dream.

You have to get help and expose the truth, Luke tells me, his voice insistent.

And I give in. I have to trust somebody. *All right*, I tell him. *But I can't do anything now. I'll get help tomorrow.* As I slide into exhausted sleep I add, *Sara. Sara likes Teddy. And exposing the truth is what reporters do. I'll get Sara to help. Tomorrow.*

Good, Luke says, pleased. But before I can relax fully into sleep he adds, *At least it's a beginning.*

thursday: false assumptions

Before I can even work out a plan for asking Sara to help me, she corners me at the lockers. "Did you hear? Did he call your father?"

My heart leaps for a second. Does she mean Teddy? But why would he call Dad? "Hear what?" I ask cautiously.

"Mr. Mitchell isn't here today." She pulls out a tissue and swipes at her nose absentmindedly. "Mrs. Feeney's trying to find a substitute."

I swing the locker door open. She's right to be curious—teachers are supposed to find their own substitutes if they're sick, not leave the school secretary scrambling to find someone at the last minute. "He didn't call in?"

Sara shakes her head, her curls catching in her glasses frames. "Everybody's talking, but nobody knows anything." She reddens as she pauses and tugs her hair loose. "Anyway, I don't believe them." Then she looks at me. "Honestly—you don't think Teddy would go off with Mr. Mitchell, do you?"

I gape at her. "What are you talking about?"

Before she can answer, Craig Leary appears, waving an imaginary microphone in my face. "Here's the man of the hour, teacher's pet and principal's son, Ian Slater. Tell us if you can, in your own words, what you know about our English and history teacher, Mr. Mitchell, and the recently lost and lamented Teddy Camden."

I shove his hand away. "What's going on?"

"May I take that as a 'no comment'?" Craig asks in his fake interviewer's voice, his hunting pack in full pursuit behind him.

"I don't have the first idea what you're talking about," I tell him, slamming the locker shut, but he won't let me alone.

"I see! So—teacher's pet and principal's son, Ian Slater, claims he doesn't know what's going on between his teacher, Mr. Mitchell, and his close friend Teddy Camden." Craig's voice turns slimy with insinuation. "Or could it be that Ian Slater knows all too well what's going on? Could it be—"

And suddenly Dad is pushing through the clusters of listening students. "What's the problem here? Leary? Having trouble finding your class?"

Instantly Craig drops the pose. "Not at all, Mr. Slater. I'm just offering Ian here some sympathy on the, uh, rather queer-looking disappearances of both his favorite teacher and his best friend." And he smiles slyly.

"Just what are you implying about my son, Leary?" Dad demands, his tone icy. One of the students behind Craig hums a funeral march, as if he's finally gone too far.

"Absolutely nothing whatsoever," Craig backpedals instantly, "except that he must be in shock at the terrible news about his old pals! It's sickening what we don't know about people sometimes."

Is Craig saying Mr. Mitchell is gay?

To my surprise, Dad seems to buy it. He's shaking his head, but he's smiling too, and Craig senses the shift, finishing, "I mean—it's too bad that Teddy couldn't find a father to take him away from this town. Maybe he ran off with his—ah—'teacher' instead."

I remember the way Mr. Mitchell barricaded himself (hiding something?) behind his desk when I photographed him. And Dad called him a sissy, and Grandmother said she wouldn't have allowed someone like Mr. Mitchell to be around impressionable young people. She wished Dad could fire him. And now Craig is implying that Teddy and Mr. Mitchell—

Except for a little nervous tittering, the hall is now completely still.

Dad says, "And I should caution you, Leary, that spreading rumors can get students into trouble." But his tone leaves no doubt that he agrees with Craig, and now that Craig isn't including me in his accusations, he's not in any trouble at all.

Dad looks at me. "Well, Ian? Aren't you supposed to be in class by now?"

I want to say something, to tell him Craig's just spouting vicious and dangerous propaganda. But no words come, and Dad hasn't bothered waiting for a reply.

He's already telling the other kids, "Go on, the rest of you, too. I don't want to see a flood of tardies on my desk because you're gossiping in the halls." Finally he turns back to Craig. "And you, Leary, don't let me hear you've been putting out any more rumors—unless they're true, all right?"

"Definitely all right, sir," Craig replies, grinning at what he takes for permission to spread this one as far as he wants.

Beside me, Sara mutters, "I don't believe it." I glance over at her. She looks bewildered. "Why did your father act like that—like *he* believed it?"

I should tell her that Dad's always right. If he believes Mr. Mitchell is gay, then he must be. Except—I'm beginning to see that Dad's not always right. If Dad thinks that Mr. Mitchell could do anything to hurt Teddy, or any student, I can't defend him to Sara, because he's wrong.

Is this what Luke means about facing up to the truth?

Once Dad's gone, Craig turns and punches me on the shoulder, grinning broadly. "Your dad's okay, man."

Craig *would* think that.

I practically sleepwalk to class. Then Mrs. Ackerman, from across the hall, comes in looking worried. "All right, class, settle down. Until Mrs. Feeney finds a substitute, I'll be keeping an eye on you." She scans the rows of students quickly and points to Sara. "You—sit up front, Sara, and keep a list of anyone who's disruptive." She turns a fierce eye on Craig and his friends and adds, "That means you, Craig Leary."

"But, ma'am, I didn't do anything!" Craig says in mock outrage.

"Not yet," she tells him. "Until the substitute comes in, I want you to get out your books and read. Sara, what are you working on right now?"

Sara doesn't try to explain our propaganda writing. "We're reading *The Ugly American*," she says.

"Fine," Mrs. Ackerman says. "Then, class, get out your books and read until the substitute arrives. I'll have my door open, and I'll be checking on you."

And with that empty threat she's gone. Craig drops his book onto his desk and makes a big show out of opening it. Sara glares at him but doesn't say anything. Most of the kids are whispering about Mr. Mitchell.

Even if Dad is right and Mr. Mitchell *is* gay, so what? There's nothing wrong with being gay. I glance again at Teddy's empty desk. But Teddy's not gay—if Mr. Mitchell's disappearance has anything to do with Teddy's, it can't be because they ran off together, the way Craig was saying— the way Dad let him get away with saying.

But Dad's got to know better. He's too smart to let a jerk like Craig take him in. Okay—so he doesn't like the way Mr. Mitchell teaches, maybe doesn't even like Mr. Mitchell himself, but Dad's got to know he's no—molester. So how could he deliberately let Craig tell lies like that, lies that could ruin Mr. Mitchell's life? What good could that possibly do anyone?

I remember watching an old movie about Lawrence of Arabia. He was this big hero, and he convinced all these Arabian tribes to work together to win their freedom. But he told a lot of lies and half-truths to do it. When one Arab chieftain caught Lawrence out in a lie, he announced, outraged, that Lawrence wasn't perfect. Lawrence thought the cause of freedom justified his lies—more propaganda.

But there's no cause that could justify Craig's lies about Mr. Mitchell. Dad is wrong this time. He's wrong.

I stare at the book, hardly seeing it. Everyone uses propaganda sometimes. I just wrote four pages of it for Mr. Mitchell. I worked hard on it—Mr. Mitchell would have been pleased. I used everything he told us: truths, and lies, and accusations and promises—everything I hear all around me—to make it convincing. But he's not here to read it.

I feel as if everyone I've come to count on is being stripped away from me, the way Dad takes away anything I own—the old toy camera, Bear. The sheriff took away my photo magazines and books and even the clothes in the hideout. Mr. Mitchell has been taken away somehow. And first Teddy disappears, then Dad makes me wonder if he was ever my friend at all.

I sit up straight. If Dad is willing to spread propaganda about Mr. Mitchell, was he doing the same thing about Teddy? Could Teddy really be the friend I thought he was?

High time you realized that, Luke tells me.

I stare blindly at the words on the page, remembering that I decided to trust him last night, and trust Sara too. Mr. Mitchell's disappearance doesn't change that. When the bell rings to end class, I take a deep breath and turn to Sara. "You want to skip lunch and go to the publications room and talk?" I hear myself ask, amazed at my daring.

She looks surprised too, then she nods. We go to the lockers, like the rest of the kids, then peel off upstairs to let ourselves into the deserted classroom.

I don't know how to begin, so I just ask, "Did Teddy ever say anything to you about Mr. Mitchell? I mean—about—what Craig was saying?"

"About his being gay?" Sara demands. "He certainly didn't! Not that it matters, of course. I mean—who cares if he's gay? It's only that I didn't know. Did you?" Then she shakes her head hard. "Of course, I'm not even sure he is. Except that your father seems to think so." She frowns.

"He's been acting strange, actually—your father, I mean, not Mr. Mitchell. Is something wrong at home?"

I swallow. He's not exactly acting strange—just acting more like his home self than his principal self. But I can't bring myself to expose him to Sara. "He's stressed out about the superintendent job," I finally say, which is true enough. Then I make myself add, "I don't know why Mr. Mitchell isn't here today, or why everybody suddenly thinks he has anything to do with Teddy's disappearance, but I know something's going on." My throat's too dry to finish, so I swallow. "And I think I know how to find out what."

She drops her backpack on a layout table with a thud. "And you haven't told anybody? I told you to tell your father on Tuesday! Or the sheriff—or somebody!"

I shake my head. "I don't know what happened Monday afternoon!"

But Luke says, *If you're going to tell her anything, tell her the truth.*

So I try. "Well, I know something happened, but I don't exactly know what." My voice trails off, and I expect her to get angrier, but she just waits for me to finish. "Have you ever, sort of, zoned out and not seen what was going on around you?"

She digs out a crumpled tissue and blows her nose, looking perplexed. "You mean like taking drugs?"

"No!" I snap. "Of course not!"

"Well..." Sara looks confused behind her purple-tinted lenses. "You mean, like being hypnotized? Doing things without knowing you're doing them, or not remembering what other people were doing while you were under?"

149

"Kind of," I say, although I have no idea what being hypnotized is like. "But without someone actually hypnotizing you."

"Well, I've heard of self-hypnosis," she says, pulling herself up to sit on the table, "and I know some people can just sort of shut out the world, like long-distance runners zoning out when they run cross-country." She sounds as if it's interesting, but fairly normal. "Is that what happened the time you acted like you'd never heard me tell you to take those pictures of the drama club?"

I let my breath out. I didn't even know I was holding it. "Exactly."

Sara frowns. "Do you think you zoned out and missed something important this time? Do you remember talking to Teddy on Monday? or Mr. Mitchell? Or maybe seeing something?"

I'm shaking my head even before she's finished her questions. "I don't know! If I missed it, how would I know what I missed? I do know I zoned out that afternoon at our hideout. It's kind of like disappearing into a fog—sometimes I can sort of see things through the fog, but most of the time I don't have any idea what's happening."

I tell her about the incomprehensible conversation with Cal, and cabin 17, and the campsite—the journals—nearly everything. "You see why I can't tell the sheriff? or Dad?" Well, she can't understand that part, because she doesn't really know Dad, but I see her nodding anyway.

"I guess they'd have a tough time understanding your seeing something but not remembering it. I wonder if you could get a hypnotist to help you remember what you do when you zone out?"

I stare at her. "I never thought of that."

"It's something to consider." Then she blows her nose and assumes her thoughtful, investigative-reporter expression. "You said you thought you could find out what happened Monday. I keep coming back to that stranger, Cal Samuels, or Clement Sawyer, or whatever his name really is, and the way he wouldn't tell you anything."

Hearing Sara put the names together, I hear how fake the name the sheriff told me sounds. And I see the connection at last. Clement Sawyer is another Mark Twain word game. Clement comes from Samuel Clemens—Mark Twain's real name—just as the Samuel in Cal Samuels does. And Sawyer comes from Mark Twain's Tom Sawyer. I'd be willing to bet that neither one is his real name. But both do have the same initials. Maybe Cal kept his real initials and made up new names that said what he wanted to say about himself. In spite of being confused and angry with him, I admire the way he did that.

"I know the evidence is all circumstantial until you can remember what happened in that blank time," Sara goes on, "but do you think Sawyer could actually be the one who did something to Teddy? He looks pretty suspicious."

Sara must see disagreement on my face. She says, "You don't think so, do you?"

"He does look like the best suspect on the surface," I admit. "Sheriff Reynolds must have thought so, or he wouldn't have gone after him." I shake my head. "I know he knows something he's not telling, and sometimes I think he has to be guilty—he sure scared me on Tuesday! But at the same time, he's got these eyes that don't look like someone who'd hurt anyone. . . . " My voice trails off.

Sara sighs. "You've got a good eye for the truth about people under their surface appearance, Ian. If that's what you think, you're probably right."

I feel an unexpected warmth inside. "If Cal really had hurt Teddy, you'd think he would have been long gone by Tuesday, not still hanging around. And if he'd wanted to, he could have actually done something to me when I found him, but he didn't."

"That's a good point—real evidence, of a sort. I just wish we had more to go on than Sherlock Holmes at Reichenbach Falls." Sara looks thoughtful. "I wonder why he's so sure you'd understand that meant Teddy was alive." She straightens suddenly. "Maybe he saw you while you were zoned out, Ian! Maybe he knows what you can't remember!" Her eyes meet mine, wide with hope. "You may not need a hypnotist after all—maybe you just need to talk to Cal."

"But I tried that," I remind her.

"You didn't tell him about zoning out, though, did you?"

I shake my head.

"Well, maybe he didn't give you good answers because you weren't very forthcoming with him," she points out matter-of-factly. "Look how much we've figured out now that you've been open with me."

She's right—and I haven't even told her everything. Maybe this is what she means about the importance of working together. Two people can come up with answers that neither one of them knew enough to piece together alone.

Sara grabs another tissue and sneezes. "Maybe he can't figure out why you haven't told anyone what you saw!

Maybe he thinks you're the one who's got something to hide, because he doesn't know you zone out. It's awfully easy to jump to conclusions—look at the way everybody's acting about Mr. Mitchell!"

"Exactly!" I can't believe how easy she's making this.

She pitches the tissue into the trash and ticks off options on her fingers. "If you don't trust the sheriff, and you don't feel you can tell your dad, and you weren't planning to talk to Cal again or try hypnosis—what *did* you have in mind?"

"I think Teddy may have written something in his journals about finding out who his father is. And—well, if there was anything to write about Mr. Mitchell, he would have written that, too." I take a deep breath. "If you came with me, we could get through them faster."

I realize why I'm telling Sara all this, why I want her to help. It's not just because Luke said I should face up to the truth. I wish I'd told Teddy more, and not locked everything inside all this time. It would be easier to hang on if I had a friend who really knew me, or at least knew something of what was going on, and liked me anyway.

"Why didn't you look at his journals yesterday?" she asks. She looks flushed and impatient.

I can't help flinching at her irritated exasperation. It's so hard to balance the truth she needs to know against the truth I can't admit to anyone, like the closet. I try to justify myself by saying, "You saw how Dad's been acting strange because he's stressed out over the promotion coming through. Well, he's wound even tighter at home, and he really blows up over totally unimportant things like supper being delayed. And Grandmother was coming over last night—that just stresses him out even more."

I expect her to roll her eyes impatiently or something, but I can see she's trying to understand. I ask, feeling my way, "Haven't your parents ever overreacted to something you've done? I mean—really gotten angry, all out of proportion? And it didn't matter if you had what you thought was a good reason or not?"

She considers this, and finally nods. "Well, I've gotten grounded unfairly, and Mom and I shout at each other over stupid things and then wish we hadn't, but that's just the way it goes." She frowns. "You mean your father would actually believe that sitting down to supper with your grandmother on time was more important than finding Teddy?"

I swallow. "Yes."

I wait for her to walk away in disgust. Instead, Sara reaches out awkwardly and pats my arm. Her hand feels hot. "I'm sorry, Ian. There I go, butting in when I should keep my mouth shut. I guess every family has its own problems."

I look up gratefully, and she barrels on, "But there's no way we can wait until after school! Look—let's cut afternoon classes and go read those journals right now."

I know I've been cutting too much—I can't think what Dad will do when he finds out—but I refuse to think about that now.

Before I can answer, Sara's beeper goes off. She pulls it out of her backpack and frowns at the number it shows. "What's Mom calling me about?"

Only Mr. Mitchell is supposed to use the phone in the publications room, but Sara grabs it and punches in her number.

"Mom? You know the school doesn't like us getting calls unless it's an emergency!" She sounds as impatient with her mother as she was with me earlier.

"What?" Now she sounds surprised—and upset. "But I can't—No, I mean it! I—But—" Apparently her mother is as bossy as she is. "You don't understand—No! Mom!" Then her shoulders slump. "All right—I'll be there. I said all right!"

She hangs up the phone, digs out another tissue, and scrubs her nose hard. "I can't believe it! This stupid cold— Mom watches too much news and she's paranoid about all these virus scares going around, so she called the doctor. She probably exaggerated all the symptoms, and the doctor said she has to bring me to the emergency room immediately." She pushes her glasses up higher onto her reddened nose and looks miserable. "She's on her way to school to pick me up right now."

"You mean your mother thinks your cold is more important than finding Teddy?" I ask, half-heartedly trying to make a joke of it.

She groans. "Ouch! Okay, you win. Parents can be totally unreasonable." Then she brightens. "But if you read Teddy's journals, I'll make my mom take me by Mr. Mitchell's house on the way back from the doctor. I'll tell her it's an emergency for the newspaper. If I behave at the hospital and let the nurses jab me with some sort of antibiotic or steroid to fight this thing, she'll do it. She knows Mr. Mitchell—we've gone there before."

"Really? You've been inside?" Since the first Halloween Dad let me go trick-or-treating (after I started school, when other kids might think something was strange if I didn't go), I've wanted to get inside that house with its terraces projecting out into the trees and its turrets stretching up to the sky like the redwoods themselves.

She nods. "It's so cool—almost like part of the forest, or a crazy tree house. Anyway, Mr. Mitchell probably has a perfectly simple explanation of why he's not in school—maybe I gave him this disgusting cold! When I get home, I'll call you and—"

"No!" I say, more sharply than I meant to.

"Why not?" she asks, looking insulted.

I stammer, "It's just that Dad doesn't want me to get calls from girls."

She sighs. "So you call me after dinner, then, okay?"

I look down. I shouldn't have told her anything after all. If I explain everything, she won't want to waste her time on me anymore, and half an explanation doesn't make any sense. Finally I think about the complaints I've heard other kids make. "Dad says I'm too young to have anything to do with girls, like dating—"

"But—" Sara's blushing now, not just from fever.

"I know it's not like that," I say quickly. "But Dad's really image conscious. Since he wants this promotion so much, he makes a big deal of insisting that I be the perfect teenager, and not date too early or anything." I don't tell her Dad wouldn't let me call Teddy either. It's too hard to explain.

She accepts the half-truth. "So that's why you're always so careful to do everything right and not get into any trouble?"

I blink, surprised that she's noticed. "Yes."

She nods. "I wondered. Some kids think you're stuck

up, but I never did. I mean—you've never acted stuck up around me. And you're such a nice guy, and a really great photographer."

"That's not me you're talking about," I tell her. "That's Teddy."

The color fades from her face and she looks more serious. "No—Teddy's a good friend, but—" She flushes, but goes on. "Well, you're both my friends, and you're both good photographers, but you're not the same. I mean—you know how a good story can make you think you're right there? Well, a good picture of a person makes you feel the way the person in the picture feels. When Teddy takes a picture, he shows me a kid, but your pictures make me feel what the kid is feeling."

She's blushing harder than ever now. Then she adds, "And—starting high school next year—well, you really are old enough to date, you know."

I feel the heat rise in my own cheeks, and wonder if she'd go out with me if I asked her—me, instead of Teddy.

"Okay, then," Sara says, all business again. She blows her nose one last time, then tosses the wadded-up tissue into the wastebasket and brushes her hair back. "Since we can't talk tonight, let's meet at my locker before homeroom tomorrow."

"Okay," I say, and realize I'm smiling. "Hey—has anyone ever told you you've got pretty hair?"

She looks up, surprised, and I add, stammering a little, "Very photogenic."

After a minute, she laughs. "Thanks, Ian. I like you too."

teddy's journal

I bike to the gas station and buy a box of heavy-duty plastic garbage bags to wrap the journals and albums so they'll stay dry. Then I set off for the campsite. I really feel strange about this. Teddy and I swore never to read each other's journal, and I'm sure he never broke his word. But I've got to know what Teddy was thinking, and the only way to do that is to see what he wrote. I just wish Sara hadn't had to go to the doctor.

No one's disturbed the campsite. I hide the bike behind the fallen tree and sit on the remains of the shattered bench. I'll just look at the last one, I tell myself. The answers should be there. Teddy will forgive me, as long as I don't look at everything. At least, I hope he will.

His journals are so different from the ones I write. I write in pencil in spiral notebooks like I use for school. Teddy uses bound books. Inside, the pages are quad-ruled in grids like graph paper. And he writes in blue ink—a long, slanting, angular hand. He started a new journal a few weeks ago, so I huddle down on the bench and make myself read that one.

Tuesday—I just can't take it anymore! Sometimes I really hate to go home. I wish I could stay in the motel overnight. If only I had electricity, I would! Some nights everything's fine—Mom and I talk about school and her work at the store, and she cooks dinner, and then we watch sitcoms on TV or play hearts or Scrabble or Yahtzee. But other nights she starts drinking as soon as she walks in the door—sometimes I think she starts before she even leaves the store! Then she's all over me—either telling me I'm rotten just like my no-good dad, or crying that I'm all she has and what's she going to do when I start high school? She goes on and on about how being bused to the high school is the first step to getting out of Sawville, and then I'll leave her and never come back.

That's what scares her, I think—that I'll grow up and leave her all alone, like my father did—worse than my father, really, because he left her pregnant with me, so she wasn't really all alone. But I don't have anybody to leave behind to take care of her. If only I knew who my father was! I've always wanted to know—just to <u>know</u>. But now I want to know for her. If I could find him, maybe I could make him help her.

I wonder if Ian knows how lucky he is, having two parents? When he grows up, he knows they can look after each other. It's not all on his shoulders. Maybe that's why he's so shy—he knows he's smart and talented and lucky with his parents on top of it! He doesn't want the other kids to envy him. Sometimes I wish we could just switch places.

Well—can't do that. So I've just got to figure out how to find a father of my own. If Ian's finished with his

journal, let's get out there and snap some shots—
photography's the best escape I've ever found.

I turn the page, feeling the heat in my face. I had no idea Teddy saw me like that—smart and talented? And lucky? Me? I shake my head. He's a good photographer, but he only saw the surface family picture. He never saw Dad tear into me or into my mom. He sure never heard Dad rip into his own mother. If I'd told him the way it really was at home, he wouldn't have wanted to switch places with me.

I can see why he wanted to find his father, though. Sometimes you just need someone to take over for you and fix things. I read his next entry.

Thursday—Last night was the worst. Mom was drinking scotch and she tripped on the carpet going into the living room, and she just lay there, crying and calling for help. What if I hadn't been there?

That settles it—I'm going to find my father. He's got a responsibility here. I can't take care of her myself forever.

But where do I start? I've asked her before, and she won't tell me. I've even asked her best friend, Carlotta Freeman, but she just laughs. Frankly, she sits around drinking with Mom a lot of evenings, so I guess she's not the most reliable person.

If anyone wanted to find out something about me, they could read my journals (not that I'd let anyone, even Ian, read them—but later on, I mean). So—did Mom keep a journal or diary or something when she was younger? If she did, she might have written in there

*about my father. Where would she keep it? Attic,
maybe? Or in her closet?*

I feel both worse and better about reading Teddy's journal after that. I'm like him, looking for his mom's diary to
read in order to find out the truth. At the same time,
though, he says he wouldn't let me read his journal—not
until "later on," anyway. Maybe this *is* later on.

*Friday—No luck looking in her closet—not enough
time to try anyplace else. And it was a good
night—Mom wanted to see my latest photos, and she
had funny stories to tell me about her customers. She
even made fettuccine and pork chops for dinner, my
favorite meal. A lot of nights we just eat takeout from
the store.*

*Mom can be such a great person—when she doesn't
drink. Sometimes I wish Carlotta wouldn't come over
so much. When she drinks with Mom, she's not good
for her. If only Mom had a friend like Ian. Yesterday I
was <u>really</u> mad at her—biking too fast on the path, not
paying attention to anything around me. Finally Ian
made me stop. He made me get off my bike and cool
down. Friends should notice when you're all knotted
up inside and need them. Carlotta doesn't notice
anything like that about Mom, not the way Ian notices
about me.*

I remember that afternoon. I could practically see steam
coming out of Teddy's ears as he stood up on his pedals,
pumping furiously as if he wanted to crash. I thought he

might hit me if I made him stop, but I was afraid he'd crash into a tree or go careening down a cliff to the river below if he didn't, so I got ahead and turned in front of him. He lost his balance and almost fell, but put his foot down in time. I thought he was mad at me because of it, but I guess he's not.

Wednesday—Bingo!!! I found her diaries in a funny round pink box in the attic. (I wonder what came in <u>that</u> box?) I found the diary for the right year and hid it in my backpack, until I had time to read it. She was kind of seeing a lot of guys . . . I feel funny reading about them, about the way she felt about them. Am I going to be like that? Dating a lot of girls, I mean, and wanting to go to bed with them? Sometimes I look at Sara and think about kissing her—but then it would just change everything between us, and I don't want it to change. Me and Ian and Sara, working on the newspaper and the yearbook together.

I remember Sara telling me what a nice guy I was, and blushing. I think things are changing between the three of us, anyway.

Mom was seventeen when she had me. That means she was only two years older than I am now when she got pregnant. She used to tell me she gave up getting her high school diploma because I came along, but it was okay because what did she need a piece of paper for? She had me instead, and that was worth it. I'm not sure whether she really means that or is just trying to convince herself.

I used to wonder why Mom doesn't ever date—maybe she had so many dates when she was younger, she got tired of it? Anyway, there were a couple of guys who were passing through—that was when the motel was still open. And there were some guys here in town. I figure it has to be one of them. That would explain why she stayed here after her parents died and she lost the motel. But she only puts down initials. That makes it tougher to figure out. But I think "CS" is the one—I just need to work out what his full name is.

Mom sounds like she really cares about pleasing him—Will CS think she's pretty enough? Is this dress nice enough for CS? Then she writes how CS was so sad one night, and it made her feel special that she could make him feel better. It almost sounds like he was nicer when he was sad—he tells her he's no good, and she's the one who's wonderful for being there for him.

When he's not sad, he doesn't seem so nice. CS was disappointed she didn't understand some political thing he was talking about, and she thought he wasn't going to want to see her again—but then he said it was okay, she was just a dumb girl and didn't have to understand politics, and she wrote she was really relieved.

My stomach cramps so hard I'm afraid I'm going to have to throw up, but I force myself to hold it in. No, I'm thinking frantically, no—he's got it wrong—it can't be—

How can I tell Sara?

CS has to be somebody else!

Friday—She keeps writing CS all the time—maybe she was being extra careful because she also writes he's a married man. But I think I've figured it out—and if I'm right, he'll work something out—he'll just have to. Anyway, I'll know for sure when I see him face-to-face and ask him.

How am I going to get through the weekend?

I flip the page roughly, almost ripping it. On the back side I see the last entry Teddy made in his journal.

Monday—I told CS I had to talk to him about something really important, someplace private. At first he tried to put me off. But then he said okay! I'm ready to explode! I can't wait to tell Ian! He's going to feel as great about this as I do, I just know it! Oh, I've just got to be right—I'll know soon.

Oh God. I think "CS" is Chris Slater. My father. I think that's who Teddy was going to meet Monday afternoon.

No wonder Teddy's calling to me in my dreams. Why didn't I tell him what my father was like? Why didn't I warn him before he went to talk to him alone?

All this time we thought we were best friends, but we never told each other any of the important things. We talked about photography and what it would be like to have our photos published in big magazines and travel all over the world—but we never talked about what was happening now. We made this pact never to look in each other's journals, but we shouldn't have kept so many secrets from each other. If we hadn't, Teddy would have known how dangerous fathers could be.

Numbly I pick up the other journal, the one I keep, its cheap wire spiral bent and twisted, the black cover bent back at one corner, the pages dog-eared. I turn to the next blank page, needing to write something, but not knowing what to put down on the shadowy blue lines that cross the paper.

I see the pencil scrawl on the left-hand page, and realize the last time I wrote in it was Monday. Was that what I was doing that afternoon at the hideout? just writing in the journal? Then why did I zone out? I stare at the scribbles, trying to find some meaning in the words.

I can't take any pictures, ever again. They can't help me now. Nothing can help.

That doesn't make any sense. I close the notebook and shove it into the plastic garbage bag with the other journals. Garbage, that's all any of them are. I don't know why I bother to keep them. I stuff the bag with the albums and the two bags of journals into the cupboard, cramming them in until they fit and wedging the door shut with a fallen branch, hiding our secrets away again. Then I get out of there, stumbling over the thick duff to the pavement, pedaling as fast as my thoughts are whirling.

What exactly happened Monday afternoon? Did Teddy tell me where he was going? Did I try to stop him? Did we fight? I can't remember fighting Teddy, but I remember the way my cheek was red and sore Tuesday morning—did Teddy hit me? Did I hit him back?

Did I push him down the drop-off?

Did I kill Teddy?

Or did my father?

Or am I wrong about CS? Relief sweeps over me at the thought. The initials aren't that unusual, are they? There must be dozens of guys with the initials CS right here in Sawville—married men, men who wouldn't leave their wives for Teddy's mother.

But Teddy wrote that I'd feel great about it. That narrows the field. Maybe he was thinking of someone else I already liked. What if CS was really Cal—Cal Samuels, or Clement Sawyer, they're both CS! Could that be why he acted so weird on Tuesday, because he didn't want the responsibility of being the father Teddy expected? Was he trying to find a way to run out on his son, the way he ran out on whatever family he had before he showed up here?

Before I can follow that line of thought, a shadow stretches out of the tall trees and turns into a striding figure. Dirty fists grasp my handlebars and wrench the bike to a stop.

"Don't you know Teddy needs you? Couldn't you even be bothered to follow up on Reichenbach Falls?" Cal shakes the bike so my teeth rattle.

"I did!" I tell him, but my voice sounds small and shrill, not defiant. "Holmes didn't die at Reichenbach Falls—the author meant him to, but readers were so upset he brought Holmes back!" I don't stop shaking even when Cal lets go of the bike. "You meant Teddy didn't die, didn't you?"

"Elementary," he mutters, folding his arms across his stretched-out sweater and frowning at me. He's still missing his coat. "Teddy made it through that first night because he was so sure you'd come. Some friend! He's still waiting."

"What?" My mind is reeling. "You knew on Tuesday—and you didn't tell me where he was?"

Cal's blue-green eyes darken like the river in full flood. "You're the one who knew firsthand, Watson." Firsthand?

He shakes his head. "I thought I could clear out on Tuesday—figured you were enough of a friend to take it from there. So why's he still waiting?"

I stare at the man's angry face. Why did he say I was the one who knew firsthand? Had Sara been right? Did Cal see what happened when I was zoned out? But why is he so angry with me? Unless—was I the one who pushed Teddy? Did Cal save him? Then why hasn't Cal turned *me* in?

"Damn it—I know you're just a kid!" I can hear the frustration in his voice. "But can't you make the hard choice and be there for your friend?" He leans forward, clenched fists swinging at his side.

What choice? I can't think—my chest tightens until I can hardly breathe. And then I'm falling away from Cal, and I dimly see him cock his head to one side before I'm sucked into gray fog, soft like duff. From a long distance I hear a voice—Luke's voice?

Leave him alone! Can't you see—he wants to make that choice, but he's not ready. He still wants to believe everything can go back to the way it was before.

What's going on? It can't be Luke—nobody can hear him except me.

Cal's voice comes from far away, almost a distant galaxy. "Who are you?"

167

Then I'm sinking so deeply into the zone that the questions fade away, and I don't care about the answers anymore.

a message

A hand on one shoulder, shaking it. I'm sitting on the duff, leaning against redwood bark, hugging my backpack against my chest. How much time passed while I was zoned out? I look around slowly, my neck creaking stiffly with the effort, and see police cars with flashing lights surrounding a bike lying on the road, surrounding a man with a scraggly graying beard, uniformed men twisting him around to snap glittering metal cuffs around his wrists beneath his tangled ponytail. I feel the hand squeezing my shoulder. "Ian— Ian!" The voice sounds thin and distant. "Are you all right? Did he hurt you?"

Inhale. Slow and deep. Now exhale. Again. When I can breathe without planning out each step, I look up to see Sheriff Reynolds' fierce eyes glaring down at me.

I blink at him. Does he mean Cal? Did Cal hurt me? I shake my head slowly.

Other voices—from back near the police cars. Luke's voice? No—no one can hear Luke but me—Cal's voice. "You've got no reason to arrest me—I didn't do anything."

Another sheriff, or a deputy, or someone. "How about vagrancy for a start?"

Cal again. "You don't understand—and you're wasting time. That boy needs help!" Teddy? But he could help Teddy by telling the sheriff's men where he is. Or doesn't he trust Sheriff Reynolds either?

They don't handcuff me. The sheriff leads me to a pickup and one of his men puts the bike in the back.

"Ian—what happened?" The sheriff's voice is hard, suspicious.

I shake my head again, still awkward, although the fog is fading and it's getting easier to move. "I don't know," I tell him honestly. I clear my throat because my voice sounds rusty. "I was biking home, and Cal was just there, and he said that Teddy made it through the first night. . . . "

The pickup jolts across the uneven seam between shoulder and roadway. "Did he tell you where he left Teddy?" the sheriff demands. I can see his hands clenched hard around the steering wheel and remember Cal's hands clenched around my handlebars. Dangerous—they're both dangerous men. I have to be careful.

"He wouldn't tell me anything specific," I say. It's an admission that I failed to save my friend, and that I might have failed him even worse.

"We'll get it out of him at the station," Sheriff Reynolds says, his voice grim. I wonder what Cal will tell him about me.

Dad thanks the sheriff for bringing me home, but once he gets me inside and locks the door he's furious. I think of Teddy's journal, fragments of a story I can barely recall now. I strain to imagine Dad and Mrs. Camden together. Could she really have been writing about him? It's easier to picture her with Cal, and to imagine him not wanting to be tied down. I can see him playing word games with her, keeping her off balance all the time, then running off when she got pregnant, not wanting to be a father.

But if CS really was Dad—did she love him, even if he put her down all the time? Did he love her? Did he ever love Mom? I wonder if he turned into someone different with Mrs. Camden than he was at home with Mom, someone he liked better.

Leaning back against the closet walls is a relief, even though he takes away the blanket tonight. I'm shaken from the afternoon, and grateful to be shut in where I'm safe to drift, where no one else can see the failure Ian, or the school Ian or the home Ian. Which one is real? It's like a triptych arrangement of photos, showing the subject from different angles so that each picture looks like another person. Are we all triptychs of different people? Dad is. I am. Mr. Mitchell, with his secrets, must be.

But then there's Sara, who seems to be the same person from every angle. The bossy, impatient, concerned journalist she wants to become is in the person she is now. Well, the photographer I want to be is in me, now, also, but there seems to be so much more crowded inside me.

I sit in the closet's dark sanctuary, praying to stay awake. I can't stand to dream about the grove again. Nothing's ever clear in dreams, and you can't apply filters or adjust the contrast or sharpen the images. But my eyelids droop and my shoulders relax against the redwood boards and I'm in the grove again. This time I see hurt and confusion on Teddy's face—his freckles stark black against the moonlit paleness of his skin.

"Where are you, Ian?" His voice is a low moan that I

can't answer. "I need you. I thought you'd always be there for me, like I'd be there for you."

"I wanted to—but I'm no good to you," I finally admit. "I tried, but I can't do anything. I'm so sorry!"

"You can!" he insists, his voice almost rising to a howl. "I'll be waiting for you—you know where."

"I don't!"

Now I'm crying, so his image blurs, but not before I see a shadowy figure moving toward him, grabbing him, shaking him.

"You have to come for me! You promised!" Teddy's voice comes in uneven jerks as his body is jolted in the figure's grasp, smashed again and again on a rocky floor until the shadow breaks him into a million pieces.

My sobs drown out any other noise, but I see Teddy falling, as if the figure has thrown him away into the trash. Then I see something falling after him—slowly revolving circles divided by spokes—wheels?—bicycle tires. He would have had his bicycle at the grove that day. That must have been what the sheriff's deputies found that made them so sure Teddy had struggled there.

I'm stumbling—running—floating across duff and pavement and grass in cloudy moonlight. I'm late, so very late. This time I've done it. How could I be so stupid as to lose track of time like that? Before I can try to slip inside unnoticed, the door bangs open and Dad towers over me as he used to when I was little. I'm hugging something, and I look down to see I'm clutching Bear against my chest, dirty and squashed and loving.

Dad reaches down toward Bear from a great height. "I told you to get rid of that thing!" he growls, a giant

Sasquatch looming out of the darkness.

But when I hold Bear out like a sacrifice, Dad doesn't take him. Instead, his forefinger and middle finger stretch out, lengthening, and I see that long nails have grown, like the long, hard nails Chinese emperors used to have. Did Mr. Mitchell teach us that? Before I can remember, Dad plunges his nails into Bear's furry face.

"No—please!" I cry out, but Dad digs until he gouges out Bear's bright black button eyes.

"I told you not to look," he says, holding the eyes out to me. "You see what I do to creatures that disobey me?"

But Bear hasn't done anything. It's all my fault. I know it—and I can see Dad knows it too. He lets the eyes roll off his palm and stretches out those two powerful fingers until I feel their nails scratching my eyelids and open them with a start.

Blackness surrounds me. I'm standing, not curled in the closet. The crisp needles of a young Douglas fir (not Dad's fingernails!) scratch my face. My legs sag in relief as I collapse to the ground, gasping for breath, tears cold on my wet cheeks. I finally get my breathing under control and look around, shivering, wondering where I am. I don't think I've ever sleepwalked so far before. I remember clutching Bear in the dream, and look down to see that I'm hugging my heavy backpack to my chest.

I make myself stand up and slide unsteady arms through the pack's straps to let it thump against my back. I have to get home before Dad checks the closet and realizes I'm not just in the bathroom. Turning away from the fir tree, I see the familiar road. But I've gone a long way. It's a good thing there's almost no traffic here at night—I was probably just walking blindly down the yellow line.

I hurry back toward the house, my bare feet cold and sore on the rough pavement. Luke is screaming at me, pummeling me with words, *Don't go back! You're out, you've got your pack with your camera and laptop—now run! Run as far as you can! Tell the counselors, tell Mr. Mitchell, tell Sheriff Reynolds, anyone, only don't go back there, ever again!*

But if I don't go home, where can I go? Who would believe me if I told them about long fingernails gouging out Bear's eyes, reaching for my own? They'd all think I'm crazy. Except maybe Teddy, if he were here.

Or maybe Cal—could I just keep going, hide in his logging cabin? Then I see stark images of the sheriff's men arresting him—the cabin's probably cordoned off with that black-and-yellow police tape, like the hideout.

Dad's house is really the only refuge I have left. As I slip indoors, I realize I had to come back, anyway. I couldn't walk out on him the way his own father left—without a word of explanation. He's my father, and I owe him more than that, even if he is CS, even if he's done something terrible.

I make myself ease the side door shut and lock it behind me. I carefully wipe my feet as completely as possible, then replace my backpack in the coatroom and creep into the closet. This time I don't have to try to stay awake—I couldn't sleep if I tried. All I can see when I close my eyes is long fingernails.

When I hear the shower I sit rigid, seeing those sharp fingernails digging into the bathroom soap. I know Dad doesn't have long fingernails in daylight—I know it was only a dream. But since my dream grove appeared in the newspaper photo, dreams seem more real than they used to.

Dad opens the closet door for me to get ready for school, and I hear Mom fixing his breakfast, hear his car starting, hear the water running to wash his dishes, hear her go back to their bedroom. Mom and I hide from each other, afraid he might return to accuse us of conspiring against him, even though neither of us has a clue what the other is thinking anymore. When did that happen? It must have been after I started school. I see faded mental snapshots: the corners of her eyes crinkling, the two of us laughing so hard that sometimes tears came. Then I became the school Ian, and everything changed.

After I hear the soft click of her door closing, I dress quickly, go downstairs, and grab my backpack. Then I stop. Why shouldn't we talk to each other? He's not even here. But I still have to nerve myself to climb the stairs again, raise my hand and knock. Beyond that door is Dad's domain, even if I know he's gone and can't come back because he has to be at school.

It takes her so long to open the door that I wonder if I really did knock. But finally she stands there, looking at me nervously, her eyes darting down the hallway to look for Dad as she clutches the throat of her robe. "He's not here," I say, and her eyes jump back to me in surprise.

"I woke up outside last night," I hear myself telling her. "I was sleepwalking." When she doesn't answer, I add, "I almost didn't come back, but I didn't have anywhere else to go."

A long silence. Then she asks, her voice so soft I can

barely hear it, "Do you think that's what your friend did? Woke up far enough from home that he decided he didn't have to go back? Do you think he had someplace to go?"

"I don't think Teddy needed to run away," I say, and she looks down, her fingers plucking at the fuzz on her robe sleeve. She doesn't ask why I might need to.

"Mom—what are you going to do when Dad gets the superintendent job?" It's been so long since we talked that it's hard to find words that say what I really mean.

Her eyes flit up to my face, then drop away. "I'll support him," she says softly, "the way I always have."

"But what about you?" I ask, almost desperately. "What do you want?"

She turns away, then. "What I've always wanted. Just to be a good wife and mother." Her voice cracks a little at the end.

I look around the unfamiliar room—Dad's room. The two beds have dark green and brown bedspreads. Dad's is neatly made already, but Mom's covers are still thrown back. They're the only thing messed up, though. The dresser is polished perfectly, the armchair in the corner bare of even a dropped sweater. Mom's sheets are scarcely wrinkled where she lay, although I can see the curve of her head etched in her pillow. She's scarcely left a mark on the room, any more than I have in the room where I used to sleep. "Do you ever want to run away, Mom?" I hear my-self ask.

Her eyes fly to mine, surprised, but she doesn't answer, just looks down again. I blink hard, staring at the dresser. Then I see it. Not something of Mom's—the redwood chip-munk I gave Dad for his birthday years ago, when I was just starting school, and trying to sort out the home Ian and the school Ian.

The world tilts and my chest tightens until I can scarcely draw breath as memories from the little-kid Ian slide over top of the present again. I'm kicking a ball in the grass beside the house. I know I can kick it straight and hard, if I just try. Other kids do it at recess. If I can learn to do it too, then I can play with them and have fun.

"There's my boy!" Daddy's voice is big and happy. I jump, because I didn't even hear the car. I was thinking too hard about the ball. He goes on, "Today's a special day!"

"Hi, Daddy." Why is it a special day, I wonder.

When I don't say more, a slight frown creases his fore-head. "Do you know what today is, Ian?"

I know I have to say something. "Are we doing something special, Daddy? Are we going to a movie?"

Sometimes Daddy and I go to see boy movies, without Mommy. We get popcorn and watch army men or sports players run around the big screen and win. Daddy likes those movies a lot. I liked it when we saw *Butch Cassidy and the Sundance Kid.* I liked the funny parts, at least the ones I understood, and I liked all the old-fashioned photographs. Daddy said it was one of his favorites and he was glad we saw it together. I think he liked it because it was a buddy story—I think Daddy wants us to be buddies who take care of each other, like Butch and Sundance did.

But Daddy says, "No, we're not going to a movie." His bushy eyebrows come closer together. "It's not that kind of a special day."

I try hard to think. School—September—all I can think about is kicking the ball straight. My eyes stray down to it, lying there in the grass, and I snap them back to Daddy before he gets really mad. "Are we going to Scotia, Daddy? Are we going out to dinner?"

"No," he snaps, and I can hear he's disappointed. But I can't think what I'm supposed to say. My foot snakes out, all by itself, and taps the ball so it rolls in a straight line until it bumps a tree root. If I could kick it like that in the playground, the other kids would clap.

"You forgot." His voice is flat, hurt. "It's nothing important, Ian—just my birthday, that's all."

It floods back to me—September! Daddy's birthday— we always make a big fuss about it! I've even gotten him a special birthday present, just from me. I saved my allowance and bought him a chipmunk carved out of red-wood, like the real chipmunks we see when we walk in the forest together. "I didn't forget, Daddy!" I say quickly. "I've got a present and everything! I was going to surprise you with it later—I promise!"

He's looking hard at me. I know he doesn't believe me. And he's right. I got the present, but I forgot today was his birthday. "Sure," he says heavily. "Sure you did, Ian." He turns and starts to go into the house. Then he stops. "What are you doing with that ball, anyway?"

I look down at the grass. "Just kicking it," I whisper. "Just practicing so I can kick it straight."

He's silent for a minute. Then he says, "Well, that's a waste of time. You're too clumsy to learn how to do anything athletic, and I guess you're too stupid to realize it."

He must be right. That one straight kick was just an accident. I'll never be able to do it again, no matter how hard I practice. I should have been getting ready for Daddy's birthday instead of wasting my time.

I put the ball away, then go upstairs to wrap the red-wood chipmunk. They put it in a box for me at the shop, and I color some paper with drawings of redwood trees, then wrap the box carefully. But the paper is stiff, and I have trouble making it wrap right. It's hard to make the tape stick.

When I give it to Daddy, he says, "Thank you, Ian. I see you put a lot of effort into this." I can't tell if he means it, or means the opposite. Sometimes he says things in a voice that tells you he doesn't mean them at all.

"It looks like you used a whole roll of tape wrapping this!" he adds, struggling to get it open. "You know, store-bought paper folds easier, so you don't have to use so much tape." I blush. He meant the opposite.

Then he laughs, and it's a real laugh. "A chipmunk—out of redwood! I can almost see him darting up a tree! Thank you, Ian. That's perfect!"

I smile at him in relief. I don't dare smile at Mommy, too. She helped me pick it out. I wanted the perfect present for Daddy, and I was afraid I wouldn't find the right thing. But if he knows I had to have Mommy's help, he'll be disappointed in me again. So I just look at him, and hope he's forgiven me for forgetting his birthday earlier.

"Ian? Ian? Are you all right?"

The voice sounds frightened. It takes a moment for me to catch my breath and find my way back to the present, and see Mom's worried face swim into focus in front of me. So many memories hitting me since Teddy disappeared—it feels as if I'm spending more time zoned out than in the present. And the flashbacks are all the off-kilter kind that

Dad would say I'm remembering wrong—that wasn't the way it happened at all. But I don't need Luke to tell me that's exactly the way it happened. The little-kid Ian inside of me knows it was.

"How can you stand it, Mom?" I ask, my hoarse whisper echoing in the nearly empty room. "How can you stand being alone all the time?"

She forces a smile. "I'm not alone. I have your father." Then she adds, "And you. And my friends."

No—Teddy is a friend. Sara is a friend. Mom doesn't have friends like that. Did she, once? "What friends, Mom? Women on committees?"

I see the image of Mrs. Camden's tears streaking her makeup the morning after Teddy disappeared. Mom hasn't answered. I look her straight in the eye—I'm tall enough. "What if you didn't have me, Mom?" I ignore her gasp. "Mrs. Camden is scared to death about Teddy—she needs a friend." I bet Mom could be a good friend, if she wanted to, but right now she only clutches her robe tighter, as if she can hide inside it. "Were the two of you friends once? Or—was she Dad's friend?"

Mom starts to shake her head, then stops. She stands there a moment, a sad look in her eyes, but she seems to be standing a little straighter. Maybe she's seeing remembered images also. Finally she says, very softly, "Suzy was my friend first."

I nod. "Well, I bet she needs a friend now." I swallow, then say the rest. "You do too, Mom. We all need friends." I want to say—friends who like us, friends who don't always tell us what's wrong with everything we do or say. But maybe she understands that without my saying it. She doesn't say she'll go see Teddy's mother, but she lets go of the collar of her robe and hugs me, tight, the way she used to do when I was just a little kid. She whispers, "It would break my heart if I didn't have you, Ian."

When she releases me and turns away, I take a last look at the redwood chipmunk. It was a good present. Dad should have been touched by the wrapping paper I colored, and pleased that Mom and I loved him so much we worked together to find the perfect gift. Then I head downstairs.

I hear it as soon as I start pedaling: a faint *whap—whap—whapping* that speeds up as I do until it's a steady clatter of little explosions like a bag of popcorn popping in the microwave. I slow down, and the whaps slow too. Puzzled, I prop the bike up on its kickstand, then step back to study it. It takes me a minute to see the source of the noise. A folded piece of grubby paper is woven through the spokes of the rear wheel so that the ends whap against the axle supports as the wheel turns.

Curious, I work the paper out from the wheel, half expecting it to be a note from Sara. I almost jump to see Teddy's slanting writing:

Ian—I've got to see you—Meet me at the Council Tree as soon as you can. You know how important this is. I need you! Please come.

My fingers close tightly around the paper, crumpling it. If Teddy wrote this, then he really is all right! He's still waiting, the way Cal said—not a body waiting for me to find it—my friend, alive, waiting for me to help him.

But—what does he mean by the Council Tree? The sense of failure weighs me down, but then I straighten. Between us, Sara and I can figure out what Teddy means and find him.

friday: counseling

But Sara never shows up at her locker to help me solve the puzzle, and she's not in homeroom. I finally go to class, hoping she'll be there, maybe even talking to Mr. Mitchell, but it's only the substitute and there's still no sign of Sara. It seems as if everyone I halfway begin to trust drops out of my life, one by one. Even Luke hasn't spoken to me since I went back last night. Who's going to disappear next?

Instead of having us continue reading *The Ugly American*, the substitute tells us to read chapter sixteen in the history textbook and answer the questions at the end. Dad must have spoken to her about curriculum. The chapter questions blur into just another obscure puzzle. I can't stop wondering about Sara. If her mother refused to take her to Mr. Mitchell's house after seeing the doctor, would she have gone by herself, maybe sneaked out after her parents fell asleep? What if something happened to her?

My stomach burns as I remember zoning out and sleepwalking last night. How long was I out? How far did I really go? Could I have run into Sara? Could I have done something I don't remember?

I have to find out what happens when I zone out—but

I'm afraid of what I'll discover about myself. I told Luke I owed it to Dad to go back to his house last night, even if he really is CS—when I zone out, how far would I go to be the son he needs? Far enough to hurt my friends?

But Teddy left me that note! I couldn't have done anything to hurt him! If he's okay, though—why hasn't he gone home? And what did he mean by the Council Tree?

I stare at the textbook, looking like the model student Dad wants me to be, as the wall clock ticks the reading hour away in slow motion and the substitute starts to drone at us about Korea and the origins of the Cold War. I can't hear her words through the buzz of questions and accusations in my head.

I see the quotation on the wall.

And this I believe: that the free, exploring mind of the individual human is the most valuable thing in the world. And this I would fight for: the freedom of the mind to take any direction it wishes, undirected.

I don't care if Mr. Mitchell is gay or straight or whatever. He wants each of us to set our mind free, free to find out what's hidden in the zone. I refuse to believe Mr. Mitchell could have done anything to hurt Teddy or Sara—even if it means I did. I refuse to believe Sara let me down. I refuse to accept there's no one I can trust—

"You—there—what's your name?"

There's silence, and she repeats the question. "You— you know who I'm talking to!"

I realize everyone's looking at me. Some of the kids are smirking, and some of them look spooked. I hear a funny, growling sound, getting louder and louder, and realize it's coming from me. "No—no—no—no—no—"

I make it stop, but I can't force any different words out, and she'll be even more furious if I keep saying "No."

"Answer me!" the sub snaps, looking as if she'll scream at me in a minute. Which Ian am I? The constant disappointment, or the perfect principal's perfect son? Neither of those Ians can answer her.

Finally Lynn says, "Excuse me, but that's Ian Slater." I guess I must be the school Ian. When the sub doesn't react, Lynn adds, "Um, he's the principal's son?"

And the sub sits back, still furious, but not prepared to shout at someone related to the principal.

Lynn goes on, "I think he needs to go to the office, you know? Or maybe to one of the counselors?" She's stepped outside of the pack, and she's trying to help me. I never realized that underneath that perfect black hair she was so brave. I guess she's got different personalities inside her, too.

In spite of the substitute's glare, Lynn continues, "A lot of students have been seeing the counselors, because of what happened to Teddy Camden, you know."

The substitute looks taken aback at that. "All right, Slater," she says finally. "Come here and I'll give you a pass to the counselor."

I don't know whether to say "Thank you" or "No—I can't go." I decide if I start saying "No" again I won't be able to stop this time. I get up, shove everything into my backpack, take the pass without meeting her eyes, and leave. No one says anything as I go out.

I shut the door behind me. The deserted hallway feels

strange, like duff slip-sliding beneath my feet, like Dad saying one of my memories isn't the way it happened. The last time I was in this hallway without a crowd of kids, Mr. Mitchell was talking to me. He wanted me to go to a counselor. I stare at the pass in my hand. It's a pass to the counselors' office. Only—Mr. Mitchell didn't sign it, did he? He's not here anymore. I'm on my own, but I'm not sure which me I'm supposed to be right now.

I shift my pack, crushed under its weight. What am I supposed to say to a counselor? What am I supposed to say to anyone? *No—no—no—no—no—*

I head toward the offices because I can't think where else to go. Where is the Council Tree?

I knock on the door to the counselors' area, off to the side of the main offices—the far side from Dad. Maybe they'll all be busy. I wouldn't mind taking a number and waiting. It might give me a chance to get my head straight. But Mrs. Voight opens the door and smiles at me.

"Ah, Ian. I've been wondering when you'd come in. I know how close you and Teddy were—this has to be terribly hard for you."

I just look at her, wondering why my feet brought me here, wondering why I should talk to her. I talked to Sara yesterday, and now she's gone.

"Sometimes when something happens to a friend, we feel guilty," she says, leading me into her office and shutting the door so no one can hear us. "We feel we're in some way responsible."

I sit down on the hard plastic chair. How could Mrs. Voight know I'm responsible? Even if I can't remember what I did, it must have been terrible to have cost me

Teddy, and our hideout, and Mr. Mitchell and now Sara—

My empty stomach cramps, suddenly, and I press my arm against it, as if I could hold in the pain. If only I knew what I'd done, and how to make up for it, I'd do it gladly, in trade for everybody else (Mom, and Dad, too) being all right. But I can't say any of this to Mrs. Voight, and I know I can't make up for what I've done, no matter how many hours I spend in the closet or how many times I say I'm sorry. And I can't escape it by running away in the night, no matter what Luke says.

No—no—there's something you can do—I don't even know anymore whether I'm hearing Luke or my own thoughts.

"That's perfectly normal, Ian," Mrs. Voight says. "When something happens to someone we're close to, we all feel we should have done something to prevent it. But that's not always true. Sometimes there just isn't anything we could have done."

I know she means to be kind, but I could have done something—I could have told Teddy what my father was like. Only I didn't. I'm responsible all right. The sheriff knows I'm guilty. He could tell her.

"Why don't you tell me what you're thinking, Ian?" she asks.

I close my eyes. I can't. I'm not allowed. Memories slide over me again, washing me into the past with the little-kid Ian who remembers everything. I'm six again, and Miss Bennett is asking if I feel okay. "Why don't you want to play kickball with the other children, Ian?"

I like Miss Bennett. I don't want to tell her, but Luke says, *Tell her. She's nice. She'll understand.* "Because I can't kick the ball hard enough," I whisper to her behind my hand. "I'm no good at it."

Miss Bennett has wavy brown hair and soft brown eyes and a smile that says she likes me. "That's all right, Ian. Everybody's learning. You'll get better if you practice."

I shake my head. "I'm too clumsy to kick the ball right. I'm too stupid to learn how. Please don't make me."

She's not smiling anymore. "Who told you that, Ian?"

I feel tears pushing against my eyelids and I blink hard, not wanting them to spill out. I see Daddy frowning, warning me not to say bad things. "No one," I whisper. "I just am."

Now Miss Bennett is kneeling beside me on the playground pavement. "I don't believe that, Ian. I think someone had to tell you that in order for you to think it was true. Who was it?"

I just shake my head.

"I think you're very bright, Ian. You're always the first one to help me put away the paints and wash the brushes, and you remember to put everything in just the right place."

You see? Luke says. *You're smart. She likes you. You can tell her.* But I still don't say anything. Putting things away right is easy to do, not like playing with the other kids or adding numbers on the blackboard.

"Ian," she says gently, "you know you're supposed to obey me in school."

I open my eyes. I do know that. "Do what your teacher tells you," Daddy says. "Do something right for a change." So Luke must be right. I nod at Miss Bennett.

"Then tell me who said you were clumsy and stupid."

And I tell her. "Daddy."

She looks at me for a long time. "Are you sure that's what your daddy said, Ian? Did he maybe say something else and you didn't understand?"

I shake my head. "I'm sorry, Miss Bennett. I don't want to be stupid or clumsy." The tears finally spill over. "I can't help it."

She takes my hand and leads me inside, past our classroom papered with bright orange pumpkins for Halloween, past the library with its picture books and stuffed animals like Bear (only I'm not a baby and I can't have Bear anymore), to the front office. She gives me a cherry lollipop and leaves me sitting on a hard bench, my sneakers dangling above the floor, while she talks to the principal, Mrs. Meade.

Miss Bennett comes out after a while and takes me back to class. She lets us color all afternoon while she reads a story about a bull who likes flowers. Then the intercom makes noise and Mrs. Meade asks her to bring me to the office again. Everybody looks at me like they know I'm in trouble, except Miss Bennett. She smiles at me and takes my hand.

I don't want to go into Mrs. Meade's office when we get there. Daddy's sitting in front of Mrs. Meade's desk. They both look up at me. Miss Bennett looks puzzled.

Mrs. Meade says, "I thought we should try to find out what's really happening here ourselves, before going outside the school system."

Daddy laughs. "I'm glad you did. Ian's not a trouble-maker, but he certainly has a big imagination."

I don't have a big imagination, do I? Isn't having an

imagination a good thing? Daddy can't mean me.

"Mr. Slater," Miss Bennett starts, but Daddy holds up one hand.

"I know how much Ian likes you," he says. "He's always telling us how nice you are to him and how much fun school is."

I must not be remembering right. I don't say anything about school at home, unless Daddy tells me he hears I can't spell or add or color in the lines.

"I'll bet he had your attention and wanted to keep it," Daddy says, smiling at Miss Bennett. "So he started making up a story and it sort of got away from him."

Miss Bennett keeps holding my hand, but she looks troubled.

Daddy looks at me, straight in the eye. "Come here, Ian," he says. His voice sounds almost the same as it did a minute ago. You have to know him to hear how disappointed it is now.

Miss Bennett lets go of my hand, and I make myself walk across Mrs. Meade's office to Daddy's chair.

"Isn't that what happened, Ian?"

Now I know I was wrong to listen to Luke. I know what I'm supposed to do. I'm supposed to be a different Ian at school—not the stupid Ian I am at home. The school Ian is a good boy and a good student. The home Ian may not be very smart, but the school Ian knows what Daddy wants me to say. "Yes, Daddy."

"Did anyone say you were stupid?" Daddy asks. "One of the other kids, maybe?"

I shake my head. "No, Daddy."

He laughs. "Of course not—you're a bright little fellow!

No one would say that to my boy. But you have a big imagination, don't you?"

The school Ian knows he wants me to say yes. He has a big imagination. "Yes, Daddy."

"You made up a story to tell Miss Bennett, didn't you?"

I keep nodding. "Yes, Daddy."

He sighs. "I guess you'd better tell her you're sorry."

I turn around, but I can't look at Miss Bennett. Now she doesn't like me anymore. I can feel it. "I'm sorry," I whisper.

Mrs. Meade says, "Well, I'm glad we got that all cleared up. Thank you so much for coming by, Chris."

"Not a problem," Daddy says. "Friday afternoon—I had things pretty much wrapped up anyway." Daddy is an assistant principal over at the middle school, but he's planning to be principal one day soon. I heard him tell Grandmother that. She doesn't believe him, but I do. "Shall I go ahead and take Ian home?"

Miss Bennett opens her mouth to say something, but Mrs. Meade says, "Why not? I'm sure you want to have a little talk with Ian."

I follow Daddy out to the car. It's sunny outside, but I feel cold, like a popsicle. He drives me home, and then he has his little talk. I don't remember what he says. I go away someplace where I can't hear him.

I spend almost all weekend in the closet. Daddy only lets me out for meals and to use the bathroom.

On Monday, when I go back to school, I'm not in Miss Bennett's class anymore. I'm in Mr. Abrams' class. And he already knows about me.

"I hear you've got a big imagination, young man," he

says. "Let's stick to the truth around here, all right?"

The school Ian nods and tries hard to look smart, but Mr. Abrams always looks at me like he doesn't believe me.

I never listen to Luke again, and he finally stops playing with me and goes away. And I never tell a teacher anything again, either. I never even raise my hand to answer questions in class.

I blink to see Mrs. Voight studying me worriedly. I've zoned out again. How can I tell her anything about Teddy and CS and Monday afternoon? What would Dad do to me now if I told?

"Ian?" Mrs. Voight is frowning. "I know this must be difficult for you, but I'm a little concerned that you seem to be drifting away, and you don't seem to want to talk to me."

She's going to tell Dad. It's Friday. I can't stay in the closet all weekend—not now. I have to find Teddy and Sara. I have to say something so she'll let me go.

The school Ian figures out what to say. "I'm sorry, Mrs. Voight. It's just that Dad wouldn't want me here, wasting your time."

She smiles. "Oh, don't worry about that, Ian. Your father was the one who insisted on counselors being available to everyone. He's quite concerned about how Teddy's disappearance is affecting the student body."

Wrong, I think. Dad's concerned about how Teddy's disappearance is affecting the school board and its decision to make him superintendent. He's only interested in the student body if someone knows where Teddy is and tells one of the counselors. And if you really want to know the truth, Mrs. Voight, Dad complains that you and the other counselors are just here to draw a big salary and make trouble for the teachers and administrators by siding with the students. So you're the last person I'd talk to.

I stand up. "No. I mean it, Mrs. Voight—it was just Mr. Mitchell's sub who sent me down here. I'm okay. But I've got to go back to class. Believe me, that's what Dad would want me to do."

Mrs. Voight looks even more troubled. "Ian, I don't think you should go—"

"No." If I just leave, all she can tell Dad is that I wouldn't talk to her. And whatever he says to pacify her, he'll know I paid attention to him: "What goes on in this family stays in this family. There's nothing we need to involve anybody else in—no problem we can't help each other deal with without an outsider's help." Even if he shakes his head at her and says he'll talk to me about it, he'll be smiling with approval inside, thinking: "That's my son. Good boy."

I'm out the door. I don't need a pass. Who's going to stop the principal's good son? I'm not going back to class, anyway. I have to go somewhere I can think—I find myself in the publications office. Teddy gone, Mr. Mitchell gone, Sara gone also—no one to bother me here. But empty silence isn't what I want—not what I ever wanted. I just wanted one friend who didn't believe I was clumsy and stupid. Teddy was that friend. He didn't think I was a failure at all. Neither did Sara. Or Mr. Mitchell. But Teddy was the first. He had the most faith in me. Apparently he still does. And I'm too stupid to find him.

No! I can't leave it at that. I won't leave it at that! This time I have to find the right answer (*expose the truth*). I can do it. I stand at the window and think how clever Teddy is with codes and word games. I stare at the trees and wonder about this Council Tree. Where does Teddy mean for me to find him?

The answer is on the very edge of the zone—I can almost see it beyond the things that the school Ian worries about, like getting good grades, like writing his propaganda. I'm sorry Mr. Mitchell isn't here to read the propaganda I wrote. I think I was convincing. When it comes right down to it, propaganda is just making people believe something you want them to believe. I know all about propaganda.

I think about the Steinbeck quote—the idea of fighting for the freedom of the mind to take any direction it wishes, undirected. That's the opposite of propaganda. If Mr. Mitchell likes that quote so much, I wonder why he's teaching us how to write propaganda? Unless he wants us to understand it so we can recognize the monsters who do monstrous things.

That thought pushes aside all the public distractions in the school Ian's mind, and I realize where Teddy is. It's not just the Council Tree—it's the Council Tree from the forest moon of Endor.

Teddy didn't give it that nickname. I did.

the council tree

I escape from school and bike as hard as I can into the forest. I remember exactly where the Council Tree is. It's the tree I photographed for my desktop picture, the one that helps me feel like a survivor. Teddy and I watched *Return of the Jedi* a couple of years ago. That was the one they filmed in one of the old-growth forests in northern California, where the Rebels went to the forest moon populated by Ewoks who lived in a village high in the redwoods.

I'd seen the movie before, but watching it with someone who loved the forest the way I did was different. I told Teddy how cool it would be to live in a tree like the survivor tree, and we named it the Endor Council Tree, after the huge tree where the Ewoks met to debate joining the Rebellion against the evil emperor.

I coast up, wheels jolting through thick duff, and jump off the bike, dropping it with a soft thump. But there's no sign of anyone else. I couldn't have misunderstood. I slide my backpack off, set it down beside the bike, and slump to sit on the woody debris. *Stupid*, Dad's voice echoes. Is he right? Is Teddy's friend Ian as useless as the home Ian? Did

I do something crazy, like imagine the note? *He has a big imagination. . . .*

Then, emerging from the burned hollow at the sixteen-foot base of the trunk, Teddy appears. He's wearing a pair of old jeans from the hideout and a T-shirt with an outsized denim shirt over it. His face is bruised and his eyes look worried, but when he sees me his grin takes over and he whoops. "I knew you'd come!"

I stumble to my feet, hardly believing my eyes. "You're okay!"

Teddy laughs. "I knew you'd find me!"

I'm so glad he's back, I want to hug him. I throw my arms around him for a minute, and he hugs me back, then we're grinning at each other like two wild men, and he lands a punch on my shoulder and we're wrestling around on the duff, laughing and nearly crying at the same time.

Finally we lie there, panting. I look at the sun slanting down through the giant redwood canopy so far above me, holding onto the forest's peace as my triumph at finding Teddy recedes. "I've been having nightmares about you," I finally say.

Teddy sighs. "That doesn't surprise me—I've been having nightmares, too."

"You should have told me you were looking so hard for your father."

He sits up and dusts the duff out of his frizzy red hair. "You should have told me what your father was really like."

I look away from him. All my agonizing over making CS fit someone else was wasted effort. CS is Chris Slater. Teddy's father is my father, after all.

Finally I whisper, "I couldn't." My voice is so low I can

barely hear it myself. When Teddy doesn't answer, I ask, "Why haven't you gone home? Your mom's been going crazy."

He stares at the Council Tree. "I know. But—if I went there, he'd know where I was. And anyway, I was mad at her." He blushes a little, making his freckles stand out. "I always knew Mom had to do it with somebody she wasn't married to in order to get me. She never pretended any different. But—that's not the same thing as meeting him face to face and realizing he hates me."

"I don't think he hates you," I say awkwardly.

Teddy glares at me. "You don't? Throwing your kid down a cliff isn't usually the way you say welcome and love you!"

I should feel horrified, but I can't help the surge of relief that sweeps over me. Whatever happened when I zoned out, I didn't hurt Teddy.

Then I see that he's waiting for some sort of explanation about Dad, and I don't know how to tell him that Dad has strange ways of showing his love. The home Ian has learned to live with them, but Teddy deserves better. If Dad wanted a perfect son, he should have realized he had one in Teddy. But I'm seeing how wrong Dad has been about a lot of things.

I can't even try to explain. Instead I ask, "Why did you go to Fern Grove with him, anyway?"

Teddy laughs shortly. "It was his idea. I thought it was so great he loved the redwoods too—like you. So I said, sure, I'd meet him there."

I remember walking through the forest with Dad, the way he explored with Grandfather. I guess it'll always be where he takes his son. But I can't understand why he said he'd meet Teddy at all. "You just came out and told him he was your father?"

"Well, not right there at school!" Teddy says, rolling his eyes and sounding exasperated. "I told him I'd found out something really important that was going to change a lot of things, and I needed to talk to him about it. He asked me what kinds of things, and I said I thought it would change his plans for a start."

I go cold. "He thought you meant he wasn't going to be superintendent next year," I say slowly.

Teddy raises his chin defiantly. "Well, Mom needs someone to look after her. I thought my father would want to help her. Anyway, after I said that, he told me he'd meet me at four in Fern Grove. He asked me if I knew where it was. I started to tell him we'd explored everywhere around here, but he just nodded when I said yes, and said he had a meeting and he'd see me there."

I close my eyes and let his words sweep over me. It must have seemed to Dad like Teddy was going to rob him of the triumph he'd worked so hard to achieve and trap him forever in Sawville. That doesn't justify what he did, but I can understand him.

My stomach clenches. Mr. Mitchell asked us: Is doing monstrous things the same as being a monster? Maybe only a monster can understand how someone can do monstrous things. If I'm capable of understanding my father, maybe I'm a monster too. When I zone out, do I turn into a monster Ian?

"But when I met him and started to explain . . . " Teddy's voice trails off, and he shakes his head, confused and angry. "He laughed at me and told me how stupid I was to think he'd believe any of this."

I feel a surge of anger. Teddy's not stupid! Then I wonder—does Dad say that to everyone? He said Teddy's mother was dumb, too. Does being around Dad make everyone's stupid personality come out? Or does it make him feel better about himself (more perfect) to make everyone else think they're smaller and more stupid than he is?

"I said I'd tell my mother and get the authorities to make him help us," Teddy says, and I can see him facing down Dad—and Dad seething like he does with Grandmother. He can't do anything about her, but he must have thought he could make Teddy leave him alone.

"I just wasn't expecting it when he grabbed me," Teddy says, shaking his head. "I tried to fight back, but he's so big! It's a good thing you and I explored this place. I knew the drop-off didn't go straight down. I caught hold of some of the ferns and swung under an overhang. I've never been so scared in my life!"

"I was afraid you were dead," I whisper.

Teddy focuses on me. "Is that why you didn't do anything?"

I want to tell him about zoning out, but I don't know how to begin. Instead, I ask, "Where did you go, if you didn't go home?"

He looks back at the Council Tree. "I got clean clothes at our hideout, but I was afraid to stay there. I thought maybe you'd tell him where it was, and he'd find me."

I flush. "I told the sheriff," I admit. "I had to."

Teddy gives me a sideways glance. "So he knows now?"

I nod, knowing he doesn't mean the sheriff.

Teddy doesn't say anything for a minute. Maybe he didn't really think I'd tell—maybe he just said that. Finally he says, his voice low, "We swore never to tell anyone."

"I didn't tell the sheriff about our journals," I say quickly, as if I can make up for betraying his hideout. "I got them out—they're safe at the campsite."

"But we don't have anywhere to go now," Teddy says softly.

I almost say that maybe we shouldn't have a hideout anymore. Maybe it's time to stop hiding what really matters to us. But that would be crazy. Everybody has a hideout.

Finally I ask, "Why didn't you go to the sheriff yourself? He's been looking everywhere for you."

"I knew he wouldn't believe me without you," Teddy says, as if this is the most obvious thing in the world.

After he tripped me up over Cal and Teddy's camera, I somehow don't think Sheriff Reynolds is going to believe me about anything, but I don't want to let Teddy down by saying so. "Where did you go, then?"

"I figured Cal would let me hide out and wouldn't ask a lot of embarrassing questions." Then Teddy frowns. "He didn't ask any questions, actually. It was like he already knew."

"I think he did," I say slowly. "I think he saw something, enough to figure it out, anyway. That would explain why he was so cryptic when I talked to him on Tuesday."

"More than usual, you mean?" Teddy asks. "After he talked to you he told me he had to clear out, and unless I was ready to talk to the sheriff I'd better disappear too."

I nod. "I warned him, but they arrested him last night."

"I know." Teddy swallows. "I saw today's paper. If he'd

left on Tuesday, he would have been okay, but he was worried about me."

We sit in silence for a few minutes. Then I say slowly, "You know, he didn't exactly tell us the truth. Cal Samuels wasn't his real name."

Teddy looks amused. "Of course it wasn't—it was just word play. Didn't you realize that?" I shake my head, feeling stupid again. "Well, once the sheriff knows the truth, he'll let Cal go. There's no law against making up a name for a joke."

I feel bad thinking of Cal in jail—and guilty for ever suspecting he might be CS. "Where did you go after that?"

Teddy's expression turns serious. "Cal left me his coat and I curled up in it and slept here Tuesday night, but it was still pretty awful. I wanted to go home, but I was afraid your dad would go after me there and do something to Mom, and I was afraid to go to the police without proof, and I didn't know what to do. So I spent Wednesday trying to think where I could hole up until I could get with you." He grins unexpectedly. "Guess what I came up with."

"What?"

"Mr. Mitchell's house."

And I have to grin back. Teddy's always felt exactly the fascination for the place that I have. We'd sometimes sneak over there to shoot photos. We kept trying to capture the whole house, but it was like trying to capture an entire redwood tree—we could only get pieces of it.

"What's it like?" I ask.

"There's a redwood growing right through the terrace!" Teddy tells me, laughing. "And you can climb all the way to the top of the turrets and feel like you're up in the trees, away from everybody. It's like being in the Ewok village for real."

The turrets were the first thing I remember seeing at Mr. Mitchell's. On Halloween he'd put candles high in the small, shadowy windows, and they'd flicker like ghost stars caught in the tree branches. Beneath the turrets, tall glass windows separated by long, straight redwood planks reflected the surrounding trees.

"The living room walls are practically all made of glass, and there's a skylight in the guest bedroom. I can see stars when I fall asleep, and in the morning it seems almost like I'm right up in the treetops, even though I know they're way far above me."

"Mr. Mitchell let you sleep in his house?" I ask, surprised. I can't help thinking about the rumors at school.

He nods. "He wanted me to go home, or call Mom, but when he saw the paper and I told him what really happened, he understood I was going to have trouble making anyone believe me. He wants me to talk to the sheriff, though. Now that you're here, we can do it together."

I still don't want to admit the sheriff nearly arrested me for withholding evidence. Instead I ask, "What made you go to Cal, anyway? I mean—you must have been—" I grope, wondering what seeing—feeling—Dad shed his public self for the first time must be like. "You must have been pretty freaked out."

Teddy nods, shuddering. He stares up into the haze around the redwoods. "You know the strangest thing? Afterward—when your dad finally left and I climbed up—everything was gone, you know? He threw my bike after me into the river, and there was no sign of my pack or camera or anything. I hurt all over, and I didn't have anything that said 'me'— any of my stuff—and I almost wasn't me anymore. I didn't have a father after all—I was nobody."

I think of everything Dad's taken from me over the years—the toy camera, Bear, the old bike. And I remember how terrified I was at the thought of him taking my iBook and my camera. Who would I be without my photographs?

Then Teddy surprises me. "It was like being born again," he says, letting that wide, free grin break loose across his face. "I could decide who I was and what I wanted, because I was—I don't know—new, somehow. I could hardly talk, but Cal doesn't make you talk if you don't feel like it. He let me just sit there, until I started to get it together. He said something on Tuesday about getting Mom and bringing her to me, if I was afraid of going to the house, but after talking to you he said we had to clear out."

He looks at the Council Tree. "If it hadn't been so uncomfortable sleeping on the ground, I might just have stayed right here, trying to get my head on straight and work out who I was, until I could get word to you." He gives me a sideways glance. "Do you know how close your Dad watches everything? I was terrified that he'd catch me trying to get you a note. I didn't know what to do, so I went to Mr. Mitchell. He always lets us think things through for ourselves, and he was so relieved to see me alive on Wednesday night, he let me stay."

He runs his fingers through the duff, then dusts them off. "And what I thought was: It's time to stop keeping secrets. I should have known who my father was from the beginning. Mom should have said. And I should have known what he was like. You should have said!

People need to know about him before they go making him superintendent."

When I don't respond, Teddy adds impatiently, "Come on, Ian. The sheriff won't believe me if I claim he tried to throw me down the drop-off, any more than Mr. Mitchell did at first. But they'll have to believe you when you tell them your father tried to kill me."

Believe me? How can I back up Teddy's story?

Everything's changed now, Luke tried to tell me. I can understand Dad wishing he could get Teddy out of the way (even if it's monstrous). An illegitimate son could make the school board members change their minds about the superintendent job. But even if what Dad did changes everything, how could I betray my own father?

Anyway, it doesn't matter, because I'm the last person Teddy wants to go with him to turn Dad in. Sheriff Reynolds won't listen to me.

I focus on that point—Teddy will understand that. "Look, the sheriff threatened to lock me up because I had your camera," I say, shaking my head and standing up. "He called it withholding evidence. And he accused me of lying because I didn't tell him about Cal the first time he questioned me. I'm the last person he'd believe!"

But Teddy doesn't understand. "What do you mean? How did you get my camera? And what does that have to do with the proof of what your father did?"

What proof?

"Ian?" Teddy gets to his feet, his tone disbelieving. "Don't you have them?"

"I—" I shake my head, bewildered. "Have what?"

Teddy looks desperate. "You've got to! Even if they

don't believe me, they'll believe you. What did you do with them?"

"That's a very good question," a calm voice says from behind us. "What did you do with—what, Ian?"

I slowly turn around to see my father standing there, still in his blue suit, his arms folded across his chest. How did he get so close so quietly? Well, it was his forest, before it was mine. And he knows every shortcut from his own father.

But how did he know where we'd be?

I don't need to ask the question aloud. Dad smiles beneath narrowed eyes. "I saw the note in your bike wheel this morning, Ian."

Of course he saw it. The home Ian nearly missed it, but Dad's way too smart for that.

"I just didn't know what Teddy meant by 'the Council Tree.' I realized it must be some code between you two, though, and I knew if I followed you I'd track him down."

Out of the corner of my eye, I see Teddy edging closer to me, away from Dad.

"You really shouldn't cut classes, Ian," Dad says, not moving. "Do you know how bad that makes me look?"

I flush and feel my stomach burning. "I'm sorry."

"Do you think the school district wants a superintendent whose own son cuts school?" He shakes his head. "All I've ever asked is that you obey me, and you've never even tried."

I can't help it—my head snaps up. I've always tried to obey him! I just can't ever do enough, or do it right. I'm not even sure how I'm failing him. Maybe I've never understood what I'm supposed to do.

"What?" Dad challenges me. "You've got something to say?"

A vague thought surfaces from somewhere deep inside me that it's two of us against one of him now—we don't have to take this. But what could Teddy and I do against Dad? There's no army of Ewoks to charge out of the trees and help us.

"What were you thinking of doing, Ian?" Dad asks. "Calling the sheriff? Do you think he'll believe anything you say after he caught you red-handed with Teddy's camera and found out you were protecting that derelict in the forest? Sheriff Reynolds will never trust a liar like you."

He's right—I've lied about everything. No one will believe anything I say now.

Dad takes a step toward me. "Well, Ian, are you going to help me?" *Yes.* "Of course you are. I'm the only one standing between you and the sheriff. Now hand over the evidence Teddy claims you have."

"I—I don't know what it is." But I'm thinking it has to be in the zone somewhere. (Is it monstrous? Does the proof condemn me as well as Dad? Then I'll just have to bear it.) *What can you tell me that will show me the way into the zone, Luke?*

Dad shakes his head. "Ian doesn't know what it is," he repeats in a mocking, whiny voice.

In one smooth movement, Teddy rights the bike behind me and mounts it.

"Stop!" Dad roars.

"Come on, Ian," cries Teddy, and his fingers close around my sleeve just as Dad lunges in, his hand outstretched.

I see long fingernails gouging out Bear's eyes, breaking the paralysis, and I turn, loop my free hand through my backpack straps, and vault onto the carrier shelf above the rear tire as Teddy hits the pedals with all his force and the bike shoots across the duff.

For one sickening moment the rear tire skids sideways under my unbalanced weight, and I'm sure we're going to fall. I glance over my shoulder to see Dad sprinting after us, one hand outstretched to grab my collar.

I balance the backpack in front of me and lean forward as Teddy shouts, "Hold on!" Then we're upright again and Teddy's weaving through trees, heading where Dad can't follow by car, and easily outpacing his running speed no matter how well he knows the trails.

evidence

Teddy coasts the bike along the gravel driveway to Mr. Mitchell's house, sunlight and shadow flickering in turn through the overhead beams of the redwood trellis. At the front door, we dismount and head inside.

"I know you know something!" Sara's voice is insistent, even though it sounds even more stuffed, and I can picture her before I see her—her hands jammed down into pockets, frowning through her glasses, the faint purple tinge making her eyes even more intense and determined.

"I don't—"

Then Teddy barges into the glass-encircled room, and Mr. Mitchell's voice dies away.

I'm behind Teddy, walking carefully on the gleaming flagstone floor. It's been waxed until it looks like the water-polished rocks in the riverbed below. I'm so unsteady that I feel I'm slipping on the shiny stones.

"What's going—" I look up to see Sara whip around to face us. Then her flushed face lights up. "Ian! You found Teddy!"

In spite of everything, I find myself smiling at her. "He gave me a clue this morning." Then I remember how she wasn't in homeroom. "But what happened? Why weren't you at school?"

Sara rolls her eyes. "Mom wouldn't let me go, and you told me not to call—the doctor said I had a temperature of 103, and Mom said I was too sick, and the newspaper and school would just have to wait. I couldn't get out until after she finally left for work—I was afraid she was going to stay home all day, but at last she said she'd just go in late. I came straight over here." She frowns. "What about you? You two rushed in here like a grizzly was after you."

Teddy looks from her to me, then up at Mr. Mitchell. "It's a long story and there's not much time." He glances back at me, and I can't meet his eyes. He says, "He saw me meeting Ian in the forest today—I'm sure he's going to figure out where to look for me."

I swallow. I'm sure he will, too. He figures everything out, in the end.

"Who?" asks Sara.

No one else says anything, so Teddy finally answers. "My father."

Before Sara can get another word out, Mr. Mitchell says, "That's it then. Teddy, you have to tell your mother and the authorities. Ian—you'd better call the sheriff and get him over here. Tell him the truth about what happened."

I just look at him, uncomprehending.

Mr. Mitchell frowns. He turns to Teddy. "You said—"

"He was right there," Teddy says, exasperated.

What is he talking about? I shake my head. "No—I was in our hideout, waiting for you."

"You followed me," Teddy says.

My mind stumbles up against that hour I spent zoned
out. I've got to find my way into the zone. *Luke? Where are
you?*

"I don't think he *can* remember what he did," Sara interrupts. "Ian and I talked about it yesterday." She flushes
a little when Teddy looks at her in surprise. "I think it's
kind of like the way a long-distance runner zones out so he
doesn't feel the pain, like going into some kind of trance.
You don't remember anything. Ian zones out sometimes.
We were talking about maybe having him explain to Cal,
or try hypnosis, but since you're here safe I guess that's not
something to worry about right now." She squeezes my
hand unexpectedly, then rushes on. "What happened with
your father, Teddy?"

"He tried to kill me," Teddy says, shortly. "My father
threw me over a drop-off into the river. He doesn't want
any illegitimate kids ruining his life."

Sara gasps and releases my hand, recoiling from his
bluntness. "Oh, Teddy—that's awful!" She blushes worse,
shaking her head. "I sound like an idiot. It's just—there's
nothing to say, but you've got to say something. I'm sorry."
Then she turns to me. "Do you think that's what you saw
when you zoned out, Ian? Could that be what you can't remember?"

Mr. Mitchell and Teddy are both looking at me, too.

"Look, Ian," Mr. Mitchell says gently, "I knew something was wrong. When Teddy came here Wednesday night
and wouldn't tell me anything, I thought I must have been
right about you two having a fight." He pauses and runs
one hand over his hair.

"Then I finally got the truth out of Teddy—and—" He

looks down, flushing. "Well, I got frightened. Your father has—" He seems to grope for words, something he never does in class. "He's made things very difficult for me these last couple of years. It was my fault, for letting him make me ashamed of who I am, but it's taken me a long time to realize that."

"You *are* gay," I say, thinking of the rumors spreading through school. Sara shoots me an outraged "who-cares?" look and scrubs at her nose with a tissue.

Teddy blinks and his chin jerks up skeptically.

The color deepens across Mr. Mitchell's neck and up into his face. "Sawville is a small town," he says unsteadily, "but my family has always lived here. It's my home."

"Sure it is," I tell him. "Nobody would care that you're gay."

"Well, I'm not certain you're quite right about that," he says, smiling faintly, "but I thank you for it."

"Of course he's right," Sara interrupts. She doesn't quite meet my eyes, though, and I'm sure we're both thinking about Craig Leary—and my father.

Mr. Mitchell smiles at her, too. Then he takes a deep breath. "I saw there was something, not quite right, I suppose, about your father when he started as principal at Sequoia—the way he'd turn on a teacher who questioned one of his decisions. It was as if he were acting like one person but hiding another." He smiled faintly. "I might not be practicing psychology professionally anymore, but that doesn't mean I can ignore problems I see. I tried to talk to him about it, to see if there was any way I could help, and he suggested we talk after school. We went for a walk in the redwoods."

Teddy looks surprised, but I'm not. Teddy—Mr. Mitchell—me—we all thought the forest was our safe haven, but it was Dad's first.

"He told me he knew all about me, about losing my job in San Francisco." The flush has faded and Mr. Mitchell looks almost white now. "There was a patient I wasn't able to help, a troubled boy about eleven years old. He said something to his parents and they—" He swallows. "They brought abuse charges against me. I never touched the boy, of course, and my lawyer got the charges dropped, but the other therapists in the practice didn't want me to stay on. And, well, I just wanted to put the whole thing behind me. I was ashamed. So I came home."

He turns toward the forest vista the glass walls expose. "Your father said it would ruin my career as a teacher as well as a psychologist if people here in Sawville knew about the accusation. He promised I'd lose my home and my job, unless I just—shut up and let him do things the way he wanted." He sighs. "I thought about leaving. But I like this house. I like living in the midst of the redwoods. So I sold out to your father in order to hold onto the things I cared about."

"Mr. Slater was blackmailing you?" Sara asks, her eyes wide behind her glasses.

Mr. Mitchell makes an awkward little shrug. "I could have trusted that the truth about the false grounds of the accusation would come out, but I knew he was aiming for bigger things than principal. I thought I could hang on and just outlast him."

I understand thinking you can hang on. It's what I've been doing for years. But now I don't know if it's any more possible to outlast Dad than it is to please him.

"Anyway," Mr. Mitchell says, "it's time I stopped trying to hang on and started doing something. If I lose my job, then I lose my job. If I have to move—" He swallows. "Well, you can't lose the memories you treasure, so I guess I'll always have this house. Teddy, you can't wait any longer to call your mother. And Ian, you've got to call the sheriff and tell him the truth about what your father tried to do to Teddy."

"Wait a minute," Sara says slowly, as if she's only now putting it all together. "Is my fever higher than the doctor thought, or are you saying that Mr. Slater is Teddy's father?" When neither Teddy nor Mr. Mitchell say anything, I nod slowly.

Sara looks struck dumb. Finally she says, her voice thin and strained, "Well, no wonder you can't remember. If there was ever anything you'd zone out and try to make yourself forget, it would be seeing your father try to kill your best friend."

With a troubled look at me, Teddy goes to the corner where the glass wall meets the stone fireplace and punches numbers into a phone on a round table of polished dark wood. He shakes his head a minute later. "Mom's line is busy," he mutters.

Mr. Mitchell asks, "Did you bike here, Sara? Could you bike to Mrs. Camden's and tell her where Teddy is and that he's okay?"

Sara nods, but she doesn't look happy about the suggestion. Mr. Mitchell adds, gently, "Teddy's mother has been worrying for too long," and that must decide her. She sighs, then goes to Teddy unexpectedly and gives him a swift hug.

He looks startled, and then blushes, but he hugs her back.

Then suddenly she's in front of me, hugging me tightly. She whispers, "I'm so sorry about your father, Ian. But you can't blame yourself if he's done something terrible, only if you don't do something now! You're not responsible for him."

I feel tears prick my eyes. But I am responsible for Dad, aren't I? Whatever monstrous things I may have done in the zone, I've never done enough to help him as the home Ian or the school Ian, or maybe it's that I've failed to help him in the right way. But I'm responsible, all right.

Then Sara's gone, and I hear the soft crunch of her tires on the driveway.

Teddy lifts the receiver and holds it out to me. "Call the sheriff, okay?"

I just stand there, blinking hard at the polished flag-stones until the dial tone disappears and the phone beeps, complaining loudly that it's been left off the hook too long. Teddy drops the receiver back into place.

Mr. Mitchell sighs and sits down in an armchair in front of the stone fireplace. He waves at a couch and some other chairs, motioning us to sit, but we both stay on our feet on opposite sides of the room.

"We seem to have some sort of confusion," Mr. Mitchell says. "Ian can't tell the sheriff what he doesn't re-member, of course. But Teddy, you're awfully certain that Ian was there. Why?"

"I told Ian I'd meet him after," Teddy says. "I wanted to talk to his father and make sure I was right, first. I didn't re-alize Ian was following me, but when I got there—when Mr. Slater was shaking me—"

I see the images from my dreams—stills, like a book where you flip the pages and see picture after picture blurring together until it looks like they're in motion.

It's time to quit hanging on alone, Luke tells me. I feel a surge of relief—I was afraid he'd gone for good after last night.

"—I looked up, and I saw the light reflect off of something in the trees," Teddy goes on. "It seemed like I was imagining it at first, but then I could hear it." He shakes his head. "I don't know how I could make out the sound with the things he was saying to me, but it was like his words blurred together, and through them I could hear this clicking noise."

Teddy turns and looks straight at me. "The light was reflecting off your camera lens, Ian. And I could hear your camera clicking."

It's time, Luke repeats—no longer trying to convince me, but confident that I already know he's right. And I do. It's past time.

Okay. I finally give permission. I feel a shudder, deep inside, as the room shifts around me. My chest tightens and I feel as if I'm sliding backward, getting smaller, as someone passes me, growing more and more real.

Mr. Mitchell starts to say something, then stops as Luke slides the backpack around in front of him and unzips it.

"The pictures," Teddy says. "They're still in your camera, aren't they?"

As if he's at home in Mr. Mitchell's tree house, Luke strides across the polished flagstones to the table where the phone sits. He deftly opens the backpack, sets out the iBook, plugs in the camera, and starts everything up.

Mr. Mitchell stands up. "Ian?" When he doesn't get an answer, he crosses the room, frowning. Slowly he says, "You're not Ian, are you?"

"What—" Teddy starts, but Mr. Mitchell waves him silent. "Who are you?" he asks.

Luke looks at the teacher and smiles. "I'm Luke." He turns to Teddy. "I took the pictures."

Luke types the password, then launches the camera software and types the extra key combination to bypass the macro that insists the camera is empty. Mr. Mitchell and Teddy watch in silence, and I watch from a distance, as if I'm outside the window, seeing the scene through rippled glass. The computer screen announces there are twenty-six images in the camera, ready to transfer to the iBook.

Frame by frame, each picture appears on the screen. The photos are clear: Dad shaking Teddy, shaking him so hard he lifts him off the ground—Teddy throwing up his arms, trying to push Dad away, twisting, unable to break Dad's grip—sharp close-ups of Dad's face, contorted in rage, and Teddy's, frightened and disbelieving—Dad banging Teddy back and forth so hard his head snaps forward and back—then Dad throwing Teddy away from him, and Teddy's body disappearing down the drop-off—Dad throwing the bike after him, one wheel spinning so that its spokes are blurred in the photograph.

Finally Teddy says, "I don't understand. If you watched it happen—if you even photographed it—" He shakes his head. "How can you not remember?" He doesn't sound angry—more as if he needs to understand.

Mr. Mitchell says, "Ian can't remember, because Ian didn't watch it happen. Luke did."

Luke smiles faintly, nodding, but Teddy looks at Mr. Mitchell as if he's crazy too.

"Have you ever heard of multiple personalities, Teddy?" Mr. Mitchell asks. "Sometimes a person, especially a child, has such painful experiences that he can't face up to them. So he separates himself into different personalities. One might be strong enough to deal with one problem, while another one comes out when it's safe. And they usually don't know the others even exist. I think Luke is one of Ian's personalities."

Luke looks out at the surrounding redwoods. "Ian saw *Return of the Jedi* a long time ago," he says, "the one filmed in the forest. I'd been around before that, but I didn't have a name until then." He looks back at Mr. Mitchell. "Ian doesn't really understand about me," he explains. "When he was a little kid, he thought I was an imaginary friend. I'm not the only one, as you guessed. There's one Ian at home, and one when his father's punishing him, and another one around school." He shoots Teddy a swift grin. "He's got a special one when he's with you."

Teddy backs away, shaking his head. "I don't believe this—I can't believe my best friend is crazy!"

"No!" Mr. Mitchell's response is immediate and emphatic. "Ian is not crazy, not at all. Having Luke and the other personalities is the only way Ian could survive."

"That's right," Luke agrees. "We each have our own role. He's even got one who holds onto the memories of when he was a little kid, and he's just starting to figure out about that one."

"Luke, you've kept the strong part of Ian safe and alive, in spite of his father, haven't you?" asks Mr. Mitchell.

Luke nods. "The Ians buy into all the crap his father dumps on him about how stupid he is. Ian doesn't want to take it, but he doesn't know how to do anything else. He wishes he could, though—so I showed up to do the things he thinks he's not brave enough to do himself. He used to like having me around, back when he treated me like an imaginary friend. But then I got him into trouble, and he sent me away. And he stopped talking to me." He sighs. "He still uses me when he has something hard to do, but he isn't even aware that he does it.

"Once Ian realized something wasn't right Monday afternoon, he let me come out and follow Teddy. But when I saw what was happening, I didn't know what to do." He rubs his cheek, although the bruise has nearly disappeared. "I almost ran away, but a branch hit me in the face and brought me back to my senses. I knew I had to think of something fast—so I started taking photographs."

"Why didn't you shout, or come help me or something?" Teddy demands. "Between the two of us, we could have gotten away."

Luke looks down. "I couldn't do that," he says quietly. "Ian's never allowed me to get between him and his father. I'm sorry. When his father lights into him, he sends me away. It was all I could do to get him hearing me again this week, and try to lead him to realizing the truth."

Mr. Mitchell sighs. "At least you can call Sheriff Reynolds and tell him," he says, "even if Ian can't."

Luke frowns. "I've been trying to make him face the truth so he'd find you, Teddy. He's starting to let me come out a little, but I don't know if he's strong enough yet to let me face someone like Sheriff Reynolds."

Teddy holds out the phone receiver. "Well, one of you has to call! The sheriff doesn't know what Mr. Slater is like!"

"I don't think anyone's going to make that call," Dad says mildly.

Mr. Mitchell whips around, clearly surprised. I feel a whooshing rush as I expand into myself again, and I grope at the edge of the table for balance. I have a hazy memory that has the unreal sense of my dreams—a memory of Luke here, in this room, actually talking to Mr. Mitchell and Teddy. Was he there last night with Cal, too?

"No," Dad says, and I blink through thinning fog to see my father standing near the hallway. Sara must have left the door unlocked. He walks across the waxed flagstones toward us. "Ian would never turn his own father in. What do you have there, anyway?"

He circles around Mr. Mitchell to glance at the computer screen. Then he turns to me, eyebrows raised. "Digital pictures? And you told the sheriff that camera was empty. You even showed him a computer screen that said so. Now how did you manage that, I wonder?"

I look down at the iBook's screen and see the series of twenty-six images from my camera—pictures of Teddy and Dad in Fern Grove—my nightmares made real. Teddy was right. I went there while I was zoned out. Or Luke did. Or we both—

"Well?" Dad snaps and I answer, numbly, "Teddy wrote a macro script for me."

"Clever Teddy," Dad says, but he doesn't sound as if he actually thinks Teddy is clever at all. "So what do you plan to do with your little pictures?"

"Show them to the sheriff!" Teddy tells him.

Dad shakes his head. "I don't think so—even Ian can't be that simple. Do you think the sheriff is going to believe in your pictures after seeing the camera was empty? It's not like a film photograph where you have an original negative, after all. With computers these days, it hardly matters what image you start with—you can change it digitally any way you like—or any way someone tells you to change it."

"Ian didn't change anything!" Teddy cries. "You know that's what happened!" He looks at me frantically. "Where's Luke?" he demands. "Luke knows!"

I blink, surprised. If Teddy knows about Luke, then it wasn't a dream.

Dad frowns. "Luke? What new story are you making up, boy?"

Suddenly I remember telling Luke I was ready to face up to the truth. He must be the one who brought up these pictures on the iBook screen—that's what he had been trying to show me all week. I've been telling myself that he's just a voice, that he can't act on his own. But of course he can—if I let him. Luke has always been part of me, hasn't he?

"Teddy's not making up any story, Slater," Mr. Mitchell says in that deceptive voice of his that doesn't seem harsh, but quiets a class of ninth-graders instantly. "He's just telling the truth—the truth about how you tried to murder him, and how you've driven your son into multiple personalities."

I stare at him. He knows about the different Ians? and about Luke? And he believes it's Dad's fault, not mine?

Dad only shakes his head pityingly. "No one's going to listen to your psychobabble about multiple personalities,

Mitchell. I just came here to get my son. But what do I find? You—a charged child molester—you took advantage of Teddy Camden's confusion and trust. You kept him here, in your house, overnight, and you molested him, didn't you, like that boy in San Francisco? The sheriff will be all too ready to accept that you're the one who's behind this, not me."

"How can you say those things?" Teddy demands, his voice high and trembling.

Dad glares at him. "I wasn't the one who plowed into your life, boy, trying to ruin everything! That was you—or don't you want to remember that part of your story?"

"I didn't try to—"

"Shut up!" Dad says sharply. "You're just a spoiled brat who needs to be taught how to behave." Then he rounds on me.

"What are you staring at?" He shakes his head. "You've certainly managed to put me in one hell of an embarrassing position this time, Ian. Do you see where your mediocre photos and your so-called friends have left you? They've left you trying to hurt me—the person you owe the most to! Who's covered for you when you screwed up? Who's sacrificed everything for you?"

I stare at him, trying to see the answer through the confusion of truths and stories mixed together in my brain. "You have," I say finally, knowing that's what Dad's son is supposed to say, knowing that on some deep level it's true.

"And how do you repay me?" Dad asks. "You lie to the sheriff, you hide evidence, you run away from me when I try to help you."

"Now wait a minute," Mr. Mitchell says, but Dad cuts

him off sharply. "You—shut up." I'm not surprised when he says nothing more.

"You don't deserve it," Dad tells me, "but I'm going to give you one last chance to be a son I can be proud of." His voice becomes calm and reasonable. "I know you'll never say anything against me to the sheriff or to anyone else." He points to the camera plugged into my iBook. "Erase those photos, Ian. And we'll say no more about it."

"No!" Teddy shouts, but Dad ignores him.

"Go on, Ian," he says. "Do it. Or are you so selfish you can't even do that much for your own flesh and blood?"

erasing the images

Teddy doesn't understand. Dad needs someone to be there for him. I've stood up to him before in little things—sneaking to the campsite behind his back, and spending afternoons in the redwoods with Teddy. But I've never openly defied him. I always knew I owed him a debt of gratitude for putting up with me, and that debt could only be paid by obedience. How am I supposed to defy him now? Without my father, I have nothing. I'm nobody.

I have Luke. . . . But I don't know what to think about Luke anymore. I need time to stop and try to make things add up, but I don't have time. I feel Teddy's confusion and Mr. Mitchell's—what? disappointment? disgust? I'm mortified by their reactions, but they're not enough to make me turn on Dad.

I know I have to obey, but I can't seem to make my feet move. Why doesn't he just do it himself? Smash the laptop? Rip the camera out of it—crush the memory chip until the pictures no longer exist, until it's only Teddy's word against his.

But no—Dad wouldn't do that. The camera cost too much money. I shouldn't have been afraid the other night that he'd make me smash it the way he made me destroy the toy—he wouldn't break this one, any more than he'd hit me so that someone could see the marks (even though he hit Teddy). He wants to keep the picture perfect for anyone who's looking. But a picture always tells the truth. You just have to look at it from the right angle, and want to see.

"You make me sick," Dad says quietly, and I want to tell him I'm trying, I really am, but I seem to have frozen between Ians—

Then Teddy lunges forward, his eyes blazing. I know I deserve his anger. There's no excuse I can make to deflect it. I bow my head, my chest aching at losing—for the second time—my friend. But Teddy doesn't lash out at me. Instead, he stands in front of me. He stands between my father and me.

"Stop it!" he shouts. His face is tear-streaked but determined. "I was wrong," he tells Dad, and his voice is hard, so hard it actually drives Dad back a few steps. "Having no father is better than having you as my father. Anyway—" His voice falters, then he makes himself go on. "I really wanted Ian as a brother, even more than I wanted to find a father. I couldn't understand why he didn't come, but now I understand all right, now that I've seen what you're really like. And I'm not going to let you treat him like that anymore."

Mr. Mitchell suddenly straightens. His face is white, except for two spots of color, high on his cheeks. "You put me to shame, Teddy," he says, each word falling sharp and clear. "I let this man blackmail me all these years—this man who tried to kill you—this man who abuses his son." He takes a deep, shuddering breath. Abuse? Dad's never abused me—just punished me because I deserved it—

What do you call tearing you down every day of your life and locking you in the closet? Of course that's abuse!

I'm not sure whether it's Luke telling me that, or the failure Ian trying to break out of the closet, or me actually thinking for myself. Mr. Mitchell goes on, "And now you're the one who has the courage to defy him while I stand by and do nothing. Well, not anymore."

Dad only laughs at him. "And what do you think you're going to do? You're the one in trouble, here with two young boys." He looks at me, straight through them, as if Teddy and Mr. Mitchell are invisible. He's not afraid of them at all.

But he should be.

Luke's right. If only I had his courage . . .

"You will do what I tell you, Ian," Dad says. "Erase the photos. Do it now."

Luke has never faced my father, and he doesn't face him now. But I feel a shudder deep inside and then he's here, turning away from Dad, toward the table, reaching for the iBook.

My hands tremble above the keys. No one has ever stood between me and Dad, the way Teddy and Mr. Mitchell are standing. Not Mom, ever. Not Miss Bennett or Mrs. Meade when I was little. But there stands my friend Teddy, defying my father, and my teacher, risking his career for me.

I think of Dad, waiting for his father to stand between him and his mother, but Grandfather never did—he left Dad all alone. He found enough courage to save himself before it was too late, but not his son. That was wrong of him—families have to be there for each other. And so do friends.

"Stop sniveling, Ian," Dad snaps, and I jump. "Erase the photos and put away your camera and laptop."

Fingers tap computer keys.

"Ian, no!" Teddy cries.

He breaks to run toward me, and Dad grabs him. Teddy wriggles in his grasp and Mr. Mitchell moves in. Dad strikes him, hard, on the side of his neck with his free hand. One final cable connection, then the last computer keys. Whose fingers hit them? mine or Luke's? I feel stretched thin, as if I'm here and I'm zoned out at the same time. Images flash around me. I see the computer screen change. I see Mr. Mitchell fall, his head striking the rough stone of the hearth. I see Teddy struggle to break away, hear him cry out, but he can't do anything to stop Dad. Only I (*we*) can.

"Are you finished?" Dad asks sharply, holding Teddy against him, one arm tight around his throat.

"It takes a few minutes," I say, turning toward him, not looking at the screen. Only the silent trees outside the glass wall watch the program run. I can't bring myself to look at Teddy, at the sudden expression of surprise on his face as he struggles to break free. I can't face his shock and—what? anger? regret for standing up for me? Later—after this is over—I'll be able to face him again. But now I just stand there, looking down until Dad's eyes break away from my face, satisfied. I count seconds. It has to be done by now.

"All right," Dad says suddenly. "It's time to wrap things up. Ian—your job is to pack up your computer equipment, if you think you're capable of handling that. For these two, I think the best thing is a car wreck on these winding roads—bad brakes, perhaps." He nods, as if confirming his plan in his mind, and I can scarcely believe he's my father. He's crossed some line and become someone else. Or maybe this is who he always was, behind the public and home personalities. "Hurry up, Ian. Help me for a change." *I am helping you, Dad.*

Images all around me—the iBook screen, Dad pulling Teddy toward the door, Luke at the keyboard, Mr. Mitchell lying where he fell. I'm glad Sara's not in any of the images right now.

You can't let him get them in the car, Luke tells me, only I know now I'm telling myself that. If Mr. Mitchell and Teddy saw Luke, then they had to see him in me. If there are Ians for school and home, and a little-kid Ian who guards my memories, then there's someone else, too—my spirit, maybe—someone I always wished I could be, someone I dreamed in Luke. And if I managed to take those photos as Luke, and managed to let people see him *(us)*, then maybe I can manage just a little more.

"You don't have to do this," I say, and my voice sounds like a stranger's voice (Luke's voice), almost as strong as Dad's. I think of Butch and Sundance—friends who stuck by each other. *Did you want someone who'd stick by you to the end, Dad? Don't worry, I won't walk out on you.*

Dad barely glances at me. "How stupid are you, Ian? You think they won't tell?"

"You're right," I tell him. "I'm stupid. And I never do anything right. I'm no help to you."

"You've got that right," he mutters, almost losing his balance on the polished stone floor as he drags Teddy, still kicking and struggling, toward the door.

I glance at the computer screen. I need to buy time. I remember the program Teddy wrote for making phone calls from my iBook. There's no microphone attached to the computer, but we don't need to say anything, Luke and I. We just need to open a line. That should get someone here before Dad can stage the car wreck. We hit the keys while Dad's cursing Teddy and the waxed flagstones.

Then we straighten and cross the room, realizing we're nearly as tall as Dad. We say, "So keep Teddy instead."

Dad stops and turns. Even Teddy stops fighting him, stunned.

"If Teddy doesn't tell, Mr. Mitchell won't," we go on, before Dad can speak. "He might even leave Sawville and go back to San Francisco. And Teddy would be a much better son to you than I am."

On the floor, Mr. Mitchell stirs. Lies, truths, half-truths, that's what he said in class. Use whatever will convince people to believe your propaganda. We can do that. We've been taught by a master.

"Teddy's strong and smart and you could be proud of him. He'd make a good impression on everyone." That's what Dad's always wanted from his son, after all, only Ian could never measure up.

Dad gives a hard bark of laughter. "God, you're stupid. You think nobody would notice?"

Teddy looks like he thinks we've flipped out, too.

Actually, why should anyone on the school board notice? They've got this image of Dad as a fine administrator with a handsome family. Teddy would fit the image perfectly. Not that they're going to have the chance to find out.

"No one will notice if you leave Sawville," we tell him, trying to sound utterly convincing. "When you take that superintendent job, no one's going to remember anything about your family—just that you have a wife and a son."

Dad laughs again. "Oh, you'd like that, wouldn't you? Having me take your friend so you can walk out on your family?"

Well, it's not going to happen like that—he'd never take Teddy in Ian's place— he'd never let us get away—but the suggestion slows him down. And that fills us with hope—hope that we can save Teddy and Mr. Mitchell, hope that we can really help Dad for once, hope that we can even find a way of helping ourselves.

"Why don't you?" we ask. "You only need one son."

Dad looks at us and shatters our attempt to work together. "What makes you think this little bastard's my son, Ian?"

"But—" Luke deserts me, and I look at Dad, stunned.

Teddy squirms, trying to get away, but Dad holds him tightly. "I read Mom's diaries," he gasps. "She said she was seeing you!"

Dad snorts, sounding almost like Grandmother. "Do you think I'm as stupid as Ian?" he demands. "I'm sorry to be the one to tell you this, Teddy, but your mother spread her legs for anyone and everyone. Even she doesn't know who your father is, I'm sure. I had a wife, and a son on the way—I took precautions so I wouldn't knock her up."

"No," Teddy tells him, trying to beat his fists on Dad's chest, only Dad has his wrists clenched in his strong grasp. "You're lying!"

I stare at Dad. "If Teddy's not your son," I say, my voice

barely above a whisper, "then why did you do it? Why didn't you just tell him he was wrong?"

"Oh, sure!" Dad says. "And have this little bastard telling lies about me, knowing some people—people on the school board—would hear sooner or later and might believe him? Knowing they'd be laughing at me behind my back while they named someone else superintendent?"

Propaganda is a blend of truths, rumors, lies. . . . But which is truth and which is lie? Before I can figure it out I hear tires screech in the driveway gravel, and the banging of car doors.

final exposure

A fist pounds on the front door. "This is Sheriff Reynolds!" he thunders, like Dad. "Open up, Mr. Mitchell! Now!"

"No," Dad orders, his voice low as he tightens his grip on Teddy.

We slowed Dad down just long enough for our plan to work. While Teddy thought I was erasing the photos, we were actually uploading them to the newspaper—and to Sheriff Reynolds. Luke had a feeling we might need his help in the end. When Ian zoned out in the bedroom Wednesday night, Luke modified Teddy's macro script. If we hit the right key combination, the iBook would send photos to the sheriff's e-mail as well as the newspaper.

But we weren't sure how soon the sheriff would see the photos. So we used the modem to open a line to the 911 emergency number for the sheriff's department. We figured they'd trace it to Mr. Mitchell's house and come check it out. And here they are.

Mr. Mitchell stumbles to his feet, staggers a little on the polished flagstones as Dad makes a grab for him, but reaches the door and opens it. I see blood on the side of his face, where he hit the hearth. Sheriff Reynolds shoulders his way in, holding up his badge. Behind him I see two uniformed deputies. One of them grabs Mr. Mitchell's arm. I can't tell if it's to hold him up or to arrest him.

"That's right," Dad says. "He's been keeping Teddy here." Somehow, his grip has changed position, so he doesn't look like he's holding Teddy prisoner anymore. He almost looks like he's protecting him. Except Teddy doesn't say anything, so Dad must be hurting him.

"We're here now, Mr. Slater," Sheriff Reynolds assures him. He glances toward me, and I see only suspicion in his eyes before he turns back to Dad. "You can let go of the Camden boy."

Dad looks from the sheriff to the two deputies beside Mr. Mitchell, then relaxes. "I don't know how you got here so fast," he begins, still holding Teddy, "but I'm glad you did. I followed Ian when he left school. That man—the boys' teacher—he's the one who—"

"I understand, Mr. Slater," the sheriff says, coming forward. "I'll take the boy now." He reaches out, as if Dad could hand over Teddy and place him in his open palm.

Before Dad can do anything, Mrs. Camden bursts through the open front door with Sara on her heels—and with my mother behind them.

Dad looks at her blankly. "Sandra?" At the same moment Mrs. Camden shrieks, "Teddy? Teddy? You're all right?" and Teddy breaks free from Dad.

The room erupts in a maelstrom of action—one deputy is putting handcuffs on Mr. Mitchell while the other comes up beside Dad. Mrs. Camden is hugging Teddy and he's crying and trying to tell her what happened. Sara appears beside me, her face white, asking if I'm okay. Through the noise and confusion I can just make out her description of her finding my mother with Teddy's mother, and Mrs. Camden calling 911 and screaming until they dispatched the deputy units to Mr. Mitchell's to get Teddy. So the clever computer call didn't matter in the end. Then Sara looks around and sees the deputy cuffing Mr. Mitchell. She runs to the sheriff and grabs his sleeve.

"It's not Mr. Mitchell you're supposed to arrest," I hear her practically shouting. "It's Mr. Slater! Just ask Teddy and Ian!"

And everything stops as Sheriff Reynolds emerges from the chaos, closing in on me. Once I thought he looked almost like a grizzly, hunched over to mask his height, but now he looks straight and tall, and forbidding.

I stumble backward, away from him, toward the table and my iBook.

He glares at me and I wonder if he's going to arrest me. Jail can't be that different from the closet. Finally he asks Sara, "Why should I believe anything this boy says? He's lied all week. I expect he'll lie again, given the chance."

I open my mouth, then close it. He won't understand.

Teddy sees the deputy reading Mr. Mitchell his rights and yells into the silence, "Mr. Mitchell didn't do anything. It was Mr. Slater! Ian saw the whole thing—tell him, Ian!" Then he adds, his voice quieter, "Or Luke—you tell them."

The sheriff turns around, frowning in confusion. "What?"

Dad steps back, holding his hands palms up as if to show his innocence. "I've been trying to find Teddy Camden as hard as you have, Sheriff. But the boy has cooked up something with my son and his teacher—"

"That's not true!" Teddy yells, but no one is listening.

"Ian?" Dad says, his eyebrows raised, as if in disbelief. "Tell the sheriff the truth now." He glances at the deputy beside him, one hand resting lightly on the butt of his holstered revolver. "I'm counting on you son." Then, in a firmer voice, "You owe it to me to explain yourself to the sheriff."

Yes, Dad, I owe it to you.

"You were there, at Fern Grove, Ian?" Sheriff Reynolds asks. "Why didn't you tell me that? Why did you lie?" His deep voice is getting angrier.

One of the deputies appears beside Sheriff Reynolds. "That's like what Sawyer told us, Sheriff. He said something about someone named Luke being there, and that's why Ian couldn't tell you anything."

So Luke had talked to Cal! And Cal tried to tell the police the truth, without being cryptic for once. It's not his fault they couldn't understand what he was talking about.

"What happened, Ian?" The sheriff asks. His voice still sounds hard, but he waits for my answer.

I try to speak, but only a croak comes out. Then Mom appears beside me and puts one arm around me, the way Dad would never let her do. "It's going to be all right, Ian," she says quietly. She hugs me firmly. "Tell the sheriff what happened."

I swallow and finally straighten to face the sheriff. "Luke followed Teddy—"

Dad interrupts, "This Luke story—Ian has a terrible imagination, Sheriff. It's in his school records. I've tried to teach him that he can't just go around making up stories, but he's a slow learner. My wife can tell you." He shoots Mom a look that orders her to agree with him, but she avoids his eyes.

Teddy breaks away from his mother and grabs the sheriff's sleeve. "That's a lie! Ian couldn't tell you what happened, Sheriff—Mr. Mitchell knows how it works." Teddy turns to him, standing there handcuffed. "Tell them about that multiple personality thing."

Mr. Mitchell looks up, his face bruised and his hair tousled. But his voice is even. "The only way Ian has been able to deal with his father's abuse is to retreat into multiple personalities, Sheriff. It's not imagination—it's a clinical condition called dissociative identity disorder." A faint shadow twists his face. "I used to be a child psychologist. It's a fairly uncommon condition, but when Ian needs to do something he doesn't think he's brave enough to do, Luke emerges. Luke was at Fern Grove, not Ian. Ian didn't know anything about it."

Sheriff Reynolds looks at me, clearly skeptical. "You expect me to buy this?"

I think of the mayor in *The Moon Is Down*, knowing the price for disobeying the invaders, but doing it anyway. Even without Luke, maybe I can be the same kind of brave as the mayor. Staring straight at the sheriff, not letting myself look at Dad, I say, "My father tried to kill Teddy."

The room goes quiet around me.

"What are you saying, Ian?" Dad asks, his voice hurt and so innocent that for a second I'm sure they'll all believe him, the way everyone has always believed him. Then I remember the pictures. "Look at my iBook."

"You didn't erase the photos!" Teddy cries, his voice

joyful. Maybe, in time, he'll forgive me.

The sheriff crosses to the table, shaking his head. "You'd better have some proof this time, Ian, because once you start lying it's hard for anyone to believe—" His voice breaks off as he sees the images on the screen.

"When you get to your office, you'll see they've been uploaded directly from the camera to your e-mail," I tell him.

After long seconds pass, Sheriff Reynolds glances briefly at the deputy beside Dad, who reaches over to lay one hand on Dad's arm.

"Hold on a minute, Sheriff," Dad says. "Digital photos can be doctored—you know that—" He turns to Mom. "Sandra—tell him I was home Monday afternoon."

But Mom shakes her head very faintly. Sheriff Reynolds nods and turns to Dad as if seeing him for the first time. "Read him his rights," he tells the deputy.

He turns to me slowly. "Ian, I'm going to have to take you into custody, too."

"Listen, Officer," says Mrs. Camden, not knowing (and probably not caring) that he's actually a sheriff. She doesn't seem drunk. She just looks tired. "You can't arrest Ian— none of this is his fault. I know what Chris Slater is like better than anyone here—except Ian and his poor mother. I should have spoken up long ago. I've seen Ian with Teddy, and I could see the marks of his father's treatment—worse than scars from a child beater. And poor Sandra—why, he wouldn't even let her speak to me! Today is the first time I've seen her in years."

She comes over to me and hugs Mom and me both, and I flush, embarrassed, but also grateful to her for putting it into words. "I know the things Chris said to me," she goes on, "the way he made me feel like dirt one minute, and then lifted up into the heavens the next because he cared enough to even look at me."

Teddy gulps. "Mom—if you knew what he was like— then how could you—how could he be my father?" So Teddy doesn't believe Dad's denial, either.

Mom gasps, and Mrs. Camden straightens up, although she keeps one arm around the two of us. "Chris Slater is *not* your father!"

"But—" Teddy shakes his head, blushing. "You wrote all about him in your diaries. . . . " It starts out like an accusation, but then his voice trails off into apology.

His mother looks at him as if she'll have something to discuss with him later, but all she says is, "I was flattered by his attention, all right? I'm sorry, Sandra." My mother just looks at Dad as Mrs. Camden repeats to Teddy, "But he is not your father!"

"But—me and Ian," he stammers. "We're like brothers."

She looks from him to me. "You two are wonderfully close—but that's friendship, Teddy. You're not brothers." She sighs and crosses the room to hug her son. "Teddy, your father was a man who came to Sawville to look at the redwoods. He stayed here for awhile and he was special to me, but when I found out I was pregnant, he left. I guess he wasn't mature enough to be a parent, and I've never really forgiven him for that—but I never regretted getting pregnant because I had you."

That may or may not be the whole story, but I feel certain she's telling the truth about Dad. He's not Teddy's father, and Teddy's not my brother. I feel strangely adrift. But then I think of Mom going to help her friend, and wonder if it's not too late to pull together the different layers of our family relationships.

Mom asks, "Sheriff, you don't really have to arrest Ian, do you?"

"I didn't say anything about arresting him," Sheriff Reynolds says quietly, not quite meeting her eyes. "But I need to turn him over to child protective services. That's the procedure in suspected child abuse situations, when one parent can't protect the child from the other." His voice softens unexpectedly. "I'm sure family services can help with counseling for you, too, Mrs. Slater."

Protective services? They'll send me somewhere else— to live with a foster family of strangers. Will the home Ian disappear if there's no home for him anymore? Who will I be then? But maybe there's another possibility.

"Sheriff Reynolds?" My voice is barely above a whisper, but he turns to me right away. "What about my grandfather? You said he was a professor. Is he still around here?" I look at Mom, and she puts her arm around me again and looks at the sheriff hopefully. "If he's willing to help us, maybe I don't have to be locked up?"

The sheriff sighs. "It's not like being locked up in jail, Ian. They'll help you, not punish you." Then he smiles. "But I think it's an excellent idea to get in touch with your grandfather. He's in Arcata, at Humboldt State University. I'll contact him myself. All right?"

I nod, beginning to see new pictures come into focus around me. "And what about Cal? Or—Clement Sawyer? You'll let him go now, won't you?"

"Yeah, Cal didn't do anything except let me stay in the

cabin on Monday night," Teddy chimes in.

The sheriff nods, and glances at my iBook. "We'll re-lease Sawyer, but I'll certainly ask him to testify. I suspect we'll need all the witnesses we can get, in addition to Ian's evidence."

I watch him striking keys on my iBook, his big hands surprisingly deft. He asks for my passwords, and I tell him. He makes a note of them, then shuts down the laptop and disconnects the camera. He's taking it all for evidence, along with me.

"Sending the photos right under your father's nose like that was really brave," Teddy says, his tone at once admir-ing and a little subdued.

"That was Luke." But it was me, too, wasn't it?

After a minute Teddy says, "I'm sorry I said you were crazy."

I shrug one shoulder, awkwardly. "That's okay. I've wondered if I was, too."

"Well, I don't understand it," Teddy admits. "But you found me, and you kept the photos safe. And you've always been my friend. I guess that's all that really matters."

It occurs to me that finding Teddy wasn't really about proving to Dad that he could be proud of me. Finding Teddy was about finding someone inside myself I could be proud of. And I think I've done that.

"So the multiple personality thing explains your zoning out," Sara says. "You don't need a hypnotist—just a shrink."

I smile a little, but I don't know if either a shrink or a hypnotist can bring my Ians and Luke together. They've helped me survive all these years, and I don't know if I'm ready to let them go yet. I think I've got to find my own way to do it, like adding layers to a photograph and then saving them all as one picture. It's the same picture it was when you started, only it has more depth.

"The sheriff's idea of child protective services is a good one," Mr. Mitchell says, rubbing his wrists where the sheriff's deputy had handcuffed him. It's funny how he acts like that hurts more than the cut on his head. Maybe it's the idea of being arrested and humiliated that hurts, not the physical injury. "They'll have counselors," he smiles at me ruefully, probably remembering his attempt to make me talk to a counselor, "and psychologists who can help you." He looks serious again. "Ian, it's important that you believe your father was completely wrong about you. He told you lies to try to make you believe you weren't good enough or clever enough to think for yourself so he could keep you under his control. Luke and the others were your defense against that."

I try to smile a little. "Propaganda resistance."

"A terrible sort of propaganda for you to have to resist."

The sheriff's deputies lead Dad across the polished flagstones toward the front door. "Ian—" Dad turns back, his eyes wide, his hands outstretched toward me, almost beseeching. The deputy put handcuffs on his wrists, but he cuffed them in front, not behind. I guess they're trying to leave him his dignity. Why didn't they do the same for Mr. Mitchell? Maybe they're still partly taken in by the perfect principal image.

"How can you do this to me, son?" Dad looks honestly bewildered. "You know I've only tried to take care of you and your mother."

Even he believes that he's done his best as a father. My memory dredges up the image of another father blinded by his own propaganda. I blink, remembering Darth Vader on the screen, urging his son to turn to the dark side of the force. I had a brave Ian before I saw *Return of the Jedi*, but he changed after I watched Luke Skywalker save the Ewoks' forest, and save his father, too. He turned into Luke, the brave son whose father might be monstrous, but was also heroic. When Luke Skywalker faced Darth Vader, he made them both whole again. Can my Luke do that for me, and for Dad?

I hear more cars outside. When the door opens, I see an explosion of lights and hear shouts.

"Great." Sheriff Reynolds sighs, frowning. "The press are here."

The newspaper must have gotten the photos we uploaded, Luke and I together. Photos don't lie. I think of how the photo of Teddy and his mother showed the love between them, in spite of her drinking and his worries about finding someone to take care of her. Watching them together today, I see how strong that bond is, how deeply Mrs. Camden cares for Teddy—not the image most people in Sawville have of her, but the truth.

I think of Mom hugging me today and trying to help Teddy's mother. I see that annual family photograph—the sad, closed-in shadow behind Mom's polite smile, and the strength in her posture, as if she could bear anything, even not touching her son in front of a photographer. I think the mother who played with the little-kid Ian is still there for me, even though she's been hiding inside herself all these years. She's starting to emerge—I think I helped her emerge. But she was there all along. If you put the different layers together, one on top of the next, they tell the truth about the person, don't they?

And what about me? Can I bring the different layers of my Ians and Luke into one picture that tells the truth about me? and about my father, too?

Sheriff Reynolds heads outside, his deputies leading Dad between them.

"Mr. Slater—have you seen these photos?"

I wonder how the reporters knew to come to Mr. Mitchell's house. Maybe they heard something on the police emergency band. But they came to find the truth.

"Mr. Slater—exactly what happened between you and the Camden boy at Fern Grove?"

"Mr. Slater—how can you explain this picture of you throwing the boy down to the river?"

More lights flash as they take photos of Dad.

"No—those pictures—you don't understand," Dad says, and I know he's stalling to come up with an explanation. He's all alone out there, with no one standing between him and their flashes and questions.

But we won't leave him all alone this time. Luke is striding to the door, and I'm with him—the home Ian and the school Ian and even the failure Ian and the little-kid Ian, and we're not zoning out. We're clustering in the doorway, together.

Before Dad can say anything else, we step forward to stand beside him. "I was there at Fern Grove," we say, and it's neither Luke's strong voice nor the hesitant home voice nor the failure's apologetic confessions, but a fusion of them all. It's a clear voice, an honest voice, like the crisp click of a camera shutter. "I saw my father try to kill Teddy Camden. I took those pictures."

We point to the camera Sheriff Reynolds is holding. "You can alter digital images on a computer, but the originals are still in that camera. They're the same as the ones you have."

Dad turns his head slowly to look at us. He looks younger, his face smooth and unlined like a sharp, clear photograph. "How can you say that, after everything I've done for you—given up for you?" He's frowning now, bewildered, and with a pang of sadness we remember his dream of being a park ranger. "You're my son. You owe me!"

We *are* his sons. And we do owe our father. Maybe the only way to help him, to redeem the monster, is to expose him to everyone, and to himself.

We face the reporters. "The photos are all true. But my father needs help."

He steps back in disbelief, almost stumbling over the deputy, who loses his balance and releases Dad's arm.

"So much for being superintendent," one of the reporters mutters.

At last!

Dad looks out at the reporters wildly, realizing he's not going to get his dream after all—he's never going to be superintendent and get out of Sawville—everything he's done has been for nothing. Then his head snaps back to us. He lunges forward, hands still cuffed in front of him. He swings his clasped fists up over his head and, in time to the rhythmic clicks of the news cameras, brings them down in a sweeping arc to crash into the side of our face.

It's been so long since he actually hit us that we weren't

sure he'd do it. But we thought, maybe, when he realized propaganda wouldn't help, he'd be seized by the same violent rage that almost killed Teddy. And if the reporters themselves took their own pictures, then surely they'd believe mine. Maybe then, instead of a trial, Dad would get the help he needs as much as we do.

Sheriff Reynolds and the deputies grab for him, pulling him off us as Mom bursts through the doorway, Teddy and Sara on either side of her. We just lie there, looking up at a sky pierced by redwood branches. When loggers cut down the massive trees, before conservation groups finally won the right to keep them safe, people said you could hear the giant fall from miles away.

The sheriff asks, quietly, "Ian? Are you all right?"

Are we? Am I? It was Luke's bravery, home Ian's and failure Ian's knowledge of their father, and school Ian's understanding of what people would see and what conclusions they would draw, that exposed Dad and made the giant fall. We all worked together for once. If we made it happen once, I can learn how to do it again.

I let the sheriff help me to my feet.

"I'm not all right yet," I tell him, "but I think I'm going to be."

about the author

Elaine Marie Alphin has been making up stories since before she could write them down. Her novels include
Counterfeit Son, winner of the 2001 Edgar Allan Poe Award
for Best Young Adult Mystery, and *Simon Says*. Ms. Alphin
also writes nonfiction books and has published more than
three hundred magazine articles. She lives in Madison,
Indiana, with her husband.